Frigid women didn't wear stockings and garters and sexy black lace bras.

They didn't travel more than three thousand miles in search of sexual release. Quinn admired Kay's courage more than he could say, and he was even more determined to help her find pure pleasure.

Quinn hauled her across the seat toward him, wrapping his arms around her. His body ached to be joined with hers. He wanted to be buried inside her until she became a part of him.

Kay was as eager as he. Her lips parted in anticipation, her breathing sped up. "And you want me?" she whispered.

He guided her hand to his rock-solid erection. "You tell me."

Then without warning, she scooted her tush across the seat until her hot body was flush with his. She pressed those sweet, honeyed lips to the pulse at his throat and lightly bit down.

"What are you doing?" His voice was so husky, so soaked with desire, he could scarcely hear his own words.

"Take me home with you," she whispered. "Make love to me right now."

He shook his head. "We can't. Because you're still not ready."

Dear Reader,

Last year it was my good fortune to travel to Alaska. Never have I been so awestruck as I was by our great forty-ninth state. On my journey I met many colorful, vibrant Alaskans. It takes a special breed to live in the land of the midnight sun, where extremes of temperature and light challenge even the most hearty souls. For weeks after my trip I couldn't stop thinking about the place.

From the northern lights to the breathtaking glaciers to the quaint little tourist towns, Alaska got into my blood. And I began to ask myself *What if?* What if there were four very handsome, very studly Alaskan bachelors who really wanted to get married but couldn't because of a shortage of women? And what if those bachelors decided to advertise for wives in the lower forty-eight states?

And so the idea for THE BACHELORS OF BEAR CREEK was born. Some of the bachelors were funny guys, some very sensual. Clearly they fit in two camps. So I wrote the books as a cross-line miniseries between Blaze and Duets. Look for *Sexy, Single and Searching* and *Eager, Eligible and Alaskan* coming in July 2002 from Duets. I can only hope I've done justice to the great land of Alaska and the wonderful people who live there!

Lori Wilde

Books by Lori Wilde

HARLEQUIN DUETS

40—SANTA'S SEXY SECRET
50—I LOVE LACY
63—BYE, BYE BACHELORHOOD
—COAXING CUPID

A TOUCH OF SILK

Lori Wilde

TORONTO • NEW YORK • LONDON
AMSTERDAM • PARIS • SYDNEY • HAMBURG
STOCKHOLM • ATHENS • TOKYO • MILAN • MADRID
PRAGUE • WARSAW • BUDAPEST • AUCKLAND

To Birgit Davis-Todd,
who gave me the chance to write about my wild, sexy Alaskans. And to my inspiration—the great state of Alaska.

ISBN 0-373-79034-1

A TOUCH OF SILK

This edition published by arrangement with Harlequin Books S.A.

Visit us at www.eHarlequin.com

Printed in U.S.A.

1

THE PANTY HOSE were killing him. Cutting his gut clean in two. Whoever invented the torturous things should be strangled outright. No mercy shown.

Sheer, black, tight. They clung like second skin to the most exquisitely shaped pair of legs he'd ever seen. Narrow ankles, smooth rounded calves, supple knees and firm thighs.

She crossed her legs and the panty hose murmured a soft whisper. *Swish.*

And what about that dark seam running up the back? Simply *sin*-sational!

Lord have mercy on an Alaskan man's soul. He'd never witnessed such sights in his hometown of Bear Creek. For a second there Quinn Scofield thought he would have to ask the flight attendant for an oxygen mask.

Boldly he peered over the top of his *Wilderness Guide Monthly* at the blond, sleek-haired, Charlize Theron look-alike. She sat in first-class seat 1B, one diagonal row up from his position in 2C. She and her dynamite hosiery, presumably on their way to JFK, had boarded the plane during the layover at O'Hare, but not once had she glanced behind her. Instead, she had been studiously typing into her laptop computer for the past thirty minutes.

This one was too cool for school and she knew it.

Polished, classy, undeniably an urbanite, she was definitely not the kind of woman he was searching for. But man, did she ever rev his engines. Without the slightest provocation, he could easily imagine those fine, gorgeous limbs wrapped around his midsection or slung over his shoulders in the throes of serious sex.

"Real hottie, isn't she?" his seatmate, a paunchy, middle-aged businessman who'd had one too many whiskey sours, slurred, and nodded at the woman.

"She's very attractive, yes," Quinn agreed, but kept his voice low so she wouldn't overhear.

Unfortunately the other man's volume control had been affected by his alcohol intake. He leaned close in a confidential manner, nudged Quinn in the ribs and winked boldly. "I'd do her in a New York minute. Know what I mean?"

Slowly Charlize turned and pinned them both with an icy glare. Quick, like a little boy chastised, the businessman looked away. But Quinn didn't flinch. He'd been dying for a glimpse of those eyes, and he wasn't going to let his seatmate's bad manners deprive him of the thrill.

Their gazes met.

And he wasn't disappointed. Her eyes were as compelling as the rest of her. Sharp, slightly almond-shaped, the color of dark chocolate.

His heart did a triple axel, then dropped, *ker-plunk,* into his stomach. He'd always had a weakness for brown-eyed blondes. Quinn smiled, giving her his best George-Clooney-on-the-make imitation.

Charlize didn't return the favor.

"Hi," he greeted her boldly. "How you doin'?"

For a minute there he thought she might speak.

Her lips parted. Her eyes widened. A hint of a smile hovered.

Come on, sweetheart, give it up.

His hopes lodged in his throat. Suddenly his imagination transported him back to the fifth grade. He remembered sneaking off during recess to play spin the bottle with his classmates in the basement of Seward Middle School with the singular hope of kissing Mindy Lou Johnson.

But then Charlize cruelly shattered his dreams. Without a word, she flicked her gaze away, as if he was of no more significance than a pesky fly, and went back to her laptop.

Snubbed! Okay, that's what he got for daring to speak to the Queen of Cool.

Quinn tried to focus on his magazine, but he couldn't concentrate. Eventually, his gaze found its way back to those legs. Eighteen months without the comforts of female companionship was a far stretch to go.

That's how long it had been since his ex-girlfriend Heather had turned down his marriage proposal. She'd told him that no matter how much she might love him, she could never be more than a fair weather Alaskan. The winters were just too harsh.

Heather begged him to move to Cleveland, but Quinn figured he must not have loved her as much as he thought. He had not yet met the woman who could convince him to leave his home. Alaska was in his blood, his heart, his soul. But man alive, sometimes those long, dark winter nights got really lonely.

Some of his friends had told him he was too stubborn, letting his love of Alaska overrule his heart. They said if he didn't learn to compromise, he'd never find true love. But others had congratulated him on sticking to his guns. He was an Alaskan man, and only a woman willing to become an Alaskan wife could make him happy.

At thirty-two Quinn was ready for a family of his own, but he knew it would take a very special lady to make her home in Bear Creek. Elegant thing like Charlize Theron there, with her fancy panty hose and her hundred-dollar haircut, would be crushed by the regal brutality of the Alaskan landscape. Nope, pretty she might be, but he needed someone tough and strong and resilient. Someone like his younger sister, Meggie. Or at least how Meggie used to be before she married Jesse Drummond and moved off to Seattle to fulfill her dream of becoming a city girl. Trouble was, in Bear Creek, men outnumbered women ten to one.

In the meantime he wasn't opposed to studying Charlize for sheer enjoyment. He tried to imagine her in Alaska and had to smile. No Broadway theater. No champagne-and-black-tie charity events for cultural enrichment. In Bear Creek if you wanted to raise money for, say, the volunteer fire department, you threw a salmon bake, got a keg of beer, slapped some hard-driving music on your CD player and let it go at that.

From where he sat, Quinn could only see her profile and those elegant hands tapping away at the keyboard. Her nose was perfectly shaped. Exquisite, in fact. Not too big, not too small. Not too sharp, not too soft.

Her cheekbones—Quinn could see just one, but he knew the other matched—were as high and sculpted as any fashion model's. Her firm but feminine chin was an artist's dream. And that mouth! Full, but not overblown like those Hollywood actresses who had their lips shot full of collagen. Lips currently adorned with lipstick the same russet shade as an Alaskan summer sunset.

Oh, this one was a fascinating combination of fire and ice, all right. Her regal demeanor shouted "You're never gonna get it," but those panty hose and spike-heeled shoes gave totally conflicting messages. Deep down she was a sensual woman aching to shake off that repressed disposition.

She closed her laptop and settled it under her seat. Her pencil dropped to the floor, unnoticed.

Quinn, never one to let good sense hold him back from something he wanted, seized the opportunity. Leaning forward, he tapped her gently on the shoulder.

"Miss?"

She jerked her head around and stabbed him with a hard, what-do-you-want-from-me-wilderness-boy expression. No doubt she was accustomed to strange men making passes at her, and she'd perfected that "hands off" look to quell even the most ardent admirer in his tracks. A necessary skill for a woman who dressed like that.

"You dropped your pencil." He pointed.

Her expression softened when she realized he wasn't hitting on her—even though he was working up to that. The corners of her lips edged upward and she silently mouthed, "Thank you."

Argh! Her simple thank-you struck like an arrow through the heart.

Yo, Mama, I think I'm in big-time lust.

When she leaned down to retrieve the pencil, she shifted her legs and her skirt rode up higher on her thigh. Quinn almost choked.

He spied the hint of something black and lacy. She

straightened, pencil in hand, and reached to tug her skirt down.

But it was too late. He already knew her secret.

She turned her head, met his eyes again and sent him a Mona Lisa smile.

Those were no panty hose.

The audacious woman was wearing a garter and stockings!

KAY FREEMONT casually took a compact from her purse.

Okay, maybe it wasn't so casually. Maybe she wanted another peek at Paul Bunyon back there without turning around and giving him the satisfaction of knowing she was interested.

Not interested in a serious way, of course. She was trying to untangle herself from an unsatisfactory relationship, not get into a new one. She merely wanted to confirm that the broad-shouldered man clad in flannel and denim was indeed as ruggedly cute as she thought.

Kay might have worried her bottom lip with her teeth, so curious was she about this man, but many years of her mother's nagging stopped her. Mustn't smear one's lipstick. Freemonts had a certain image to maintain.

She feigned using the compact mirror to pat her unmussed hair into place, but she angled it so she could see him. Secretly she'd always been sexually attracted to burly, outdoorsy men. Strong, physical men who played contact sports and repaired their own cars. Men who chopped wood and roasted raw meat over fire pits. Men who'd fight to the death to protect their women.

The fact that her boyfriend Lloyd was a slender,

brainy, pacifistic vegetarian who didn't even own a car, much less know how to work on one, did not escape her. But just because she daydreamed about extremely manly men didn't mean she coveted a relationship with one. It was simply a sexual fantasy.

Besides some things were more important than sex. Companionship, for instance.

And Lloyd is such a great companion? He works eighty-hour weeks. And when was the last time he made love to you? Seven, eight weeks ago?

That wasn't fair. She couldn't lay blame solely at his feet. She was as busy as Lloyd.

And is it your fault that Lloyd has never satisfied you in bed?

Maybe it *was* her fault. Even though she spent a lot of time researching and writing how-to-improve-your-sex-life articles like "How to Achieve Multiple Orgasms" and "Tantric Sex, The New Revolution in Intimacy," for the hottest women's magazine in the country, Kay had yet to experience such lofty sensations herself.

Yes, she read and she read and she read. From classics like *The Hite Report* and *The Story of O* to the most up-to-date literature on the subject, she knew them all by heart. Kay understood the mechanics of sex, and she kept thinking that if she just gathered enough knowledge on the subject, one day she'd be able to scale her way to the stars.

Maybe she should see a counselor, instead.

Or maybe you should just have a wild, uninhibited fling. I bet Paul Bunyon's got what it takes to please a woman. Did you get a load of those hands? If it's true what they say about the size of a man's hands and the size of his…

Kay tilted the mirror to the right to get a better look.

Paul Bunyon's upper arms were as big as her thighs. For some illogical reason, this thought made her shiver. He was so very large and seemed to be constructed of pure steel. He was tall and muscular and solid. She imagined he could toss her over his shoulder more easily than she could pick up a tea bag. He possessed hair the color of aged whiskey and sultry gray eyes that snapped with surprising intelligence.

His shirt was a comforting shade of blue, and he had the sleeves rolled up a quarter turn, giving her a peek of sexy forearms offset by a thick, leather-banded watch. Nice. Very nice. Just the right amount of hair. Kay had a weakness for sexy forearms.

She licked her lips, forgetting all about smearing her lipstick. A weighted feeling settled over her and made her blood flow hot and sluggish as the erotic sensation drifted down to wedge heavily between her legs. She wondered what would happen if she stood up and walked toward him. What would he do if she bent down to his ear and with a seductive whisper invited him to become a member of the mile-high club with her? Tingles dove down her spine.

If she pivoted on her heel and sashayed to the lavatory, would he follow?

She swallowed hard past the lump in her throat. What a tight fit! The two of them crammed into an airplane lavatory. It would require some maneuvering. Kay stared so hard into the mirror of her compact that her vision blurred and she was transported.

He lifts her up on the counter; his eyes fill with heated desire. He takes one of those big hands and, starting at her right ankle, he oh-so-slowly moves it up her leg, past the curve of her calf, to the bend of her knee. She gasps at his touch. His callused fingertips snag her stockings, tearing them until she resembles a lady of the evening after a long night of selling pleasure.

Then his other hand starts its journey up her left leg. He moves closer, and she wraps her legs around his waist. The top of her head is resting against the restroom mirror, and her back is arched. He stares into her eyes, captivated. Clearly he thinks she is the most exquisite creature on the face of the earth.

His right hand goes farther. Moving up her knee inch by inch. Her skirt hikes high. The sensations are incredible. His rough fingers sliding over her bare skin, the cold sink beneath her bottom, the feel of his hard waist against the inside of her legs. She feels a million things at once, and they are all good.

He's still looking at her, but not saying a single word. He smells delicious, like Christmas trees and woodsmoke and leather. She feels herself moisten with desire. She wants him like a lion wants a lamb.

"Kiss me," she commands him in a bossy voice.

He dips his head. His hands are on her thighs, palms splayed. He's so close, but he doesn't lower his lips to hers. He's teasing. There's a naughty gleam in his eye.

"What will you give me for a kiss?" he asks.

His voice is heart-stoppingly sexy. A resonant sound that fills her ears like the loveliest bass instrument. Her pulse throbs at her throat. She's hot all over. Hot and wet and desperate.

"I'll give you whatever you want," she whimpers.

"I want you to touch me," he says. "Here."

And then he takes her hand and guides it to the bulge straining against the zipper of his blue jeans.

She eases down the zipper, slips her hand inside. He's going commando, no underwear. She touches him.

It's so big. So hard. So hot. Scalding. He smells of musky male, and her excitement escalates. He groans and closes his eyes.

At the same time as she's touching him, his hand is busy snaking up her thigh to hook a finger around the waistband of her panties.

She moans. He crushes his mouth to hers.

He tastes too good to be true. Not the finest caviar in her mother's pantry, not even the most expensive bottle of French champagne in her father's cellar can compete with his flavor.

Her palm is pressed hard against his erection, which seems to keep growing and growing and growing. His tongue is a menace, dazzling her with moves she never thought possible.

"I want you inside me."

"No. Not yet. First, I'm going to make you beg."

She whimpers again.

"That's right." He nods. "This has been a long time coming."

Her nipples tighten. She wriggles her hips. Her panties are whisked off.

"What are you doing?"

"Hush, woman," he growls. "Hush and enjoy. You deserve everything I'm going to give you and so much more. You drive me wild."

She glows at his words. Men have told her she's beautiful before, but no one has ever told her she drives him wild. He's telling her exactly what she needs to hear, and she loves him for it. She feels incredibly powerful that she's controlling such a big man with her sexuality.

Then he goes to work with his fingers.

He's stroking her inner thigh, and then he trails his fingertips inward. He's doing something that makes her eyes roll back in her head with sheer ecstasy.

Oh, gawd, what that intoxicating hand is doing at the apex of her womanhood!

She writhes against him, clutches his shoulders with both hands, digs her fingers into his flesh through the soft flannel of his shirt.

His movements are gentle but firm. The pressure builds. No man has ever caressed her in quite this way. It's as if he knows exactly how to make her cry out for more. She's never been this excited, this desperate, this famished for a man's body.

"Don't stop," she pleads.

He grins. For a moment she fears he'll stop simply to taunt her. But to her relief he keeps going. And going. And going.

She feels as if she's riding a roller coaster. Chugging up, up, up. Breath held in anticipation of the rapturous plunge.

She's close. So very close. Teetering on the verge. One more second. Oh, yes. Yes. She's just about to—

"Miss?" The flight attendant's voice slammed her rudely back to earth.

"Yes," Kay gasped, feeling breathless, edgy and achy.

"Would you care for another beverage?"

She shook her head. The flight attendant moved on down the aisle. Then Kay realized she was still holding the compact. She glanced into the mirror one last time and was horrified to see Paul Bunyon staring right at her.

Their eyes met in the mirror's reflection. Her heart

raced. Her mouth went dry. He gave her a cocksure smile as if he knew exactly what she'd been thinking.

Flushed and flustered, Kay snapped the compact closed and dropped it into her purse. She burned weak, shaky, her entire body swamped in heat. This wouldn't do. She had to compose herself. Immediately, if not sooner.

Unbuckling her seat belt, she got up, slipped into the lavatory and locked the door. Bad idea. This was the scene of the fictitious crime, and she couldn't escape her own mind.

She wet a paper towel, pressed it first to the back of her neck, then to the hollow of her throat and took several long, slow, deep breaths. For the past few months she'd been plagued by uncontrollable sexual fantasies. It was quite embarrassing, really. As if she was some kind of X-rated, female Walter Mitty.

Perhaps a fling was in order. Find someone to pop her cork, as it were. Perhaps that would put an end to these persistent flights of sexual fancy.

Kay pinched the bridge of her nose to ward off more blushing. This was simply ridiculous. She had to stop entertaining such unsuitable thoughts about total strangers. She took several more deep breaths, tossed the damp towel into the trash, then ran her fingers through her hair. There. She looked fine. Perfectly normal. Perfectly in control. No one would suspect anything to the contrary.

The plane lurched, jostling her as she unlocked the accordion-style door and tried to shove it open, but the silly thing stuck.

The plane pitched again, throwing Kay forward. She

put a hand on the door hinges to brace herself, and the door folded open. She raised her head in alarm.

And found herself tumbling headlong into Paul Bunyon's arms, as if he'd been waiting outside the door just to catch her when she fell.

2

"WHY, HELLO." Quinn smiled down into the face of a goddess.

What compelled him to trail her to the lavatory, he couldn't say. Maybe it was that sassy, controlled walk of hers that hypnotized him. Maybe it was her contradictory aura, pushing and pulling him in two different directions. Or maybe it was plain old horniness on his part.

But now he sure was glad he'd followed her. If he hadn't been there to catch her, she would have pitched head first into the bulkhead opposite the lavatory and bruised her pretty face, and that would have been a crying shame.

"Are you all right?" he asked.

"Fine," she whispered.

Her voice surprised him. One more irreconcilable fact that added to her allure. He'd expected her tone would be more cultured, aloof, cool and reserved. Instead, the sexy sound of her had him remembering all those nights during high school and college that he'd spun records of throaty-voiced female blues singers at his family's tiny radio station in Bear Creek.

Unblinking, the goddess met his gaze and held it. The impact slugged him. Her sultry eyes, dark as coffee and surrounded by lashes as impossibly thick as paintbrushes, snagged something deep inside him and refused to let go.

In the brief, endless moment he held her in his arms, he noticed everything about her.

The tiny mole at the left corner of her mouth. The smooth, expertly penciled arch of her brow. The erratic throbbing of her pulse in the hollow of her neck. The slim curve of her waist. Her rich, fresh scent that made him ache to bury his nose in her hair and breathe deeply.

And the unnerving realization that beneath her ultrasoft silk blouse and bra, her nipples were puckered.

It wasn't cold in the plane's cramped confines. In fact, it was very, very hot.

Had her breasts hardened in response to him? Quinn almost groaned aloud at the thought.

Was he reading too much into this casual encounter? Was his desire for one last fiery sexual adventure before he found a wife and settled down for good feeding into his imagination and causing him to misread her reaction?

Her lips parted, and he could see the pink tip of her tongue pressing against her top teeth. She looked as if she might say something to him, but she didn't.

Oh, Lord, he could feel her stockings rub against the leg of his jeans as she shifted in his arms.

So many thoughts raced through his brain it seemed as if eons had passed. But it couldn't have been more than a few seconds since she'd toppled into his embrace.

She raised a hand to her cheek to brush away a strand of golden hair. He tracked her movement, peered into those compelling brown eyes once more.

And stumbled. Literally lost his balance as the plane

hit another pocket of turbulence. He tipped backward, taking Charlize with him.

They ended up in the middle of the aisle, a jumble of arms and legs. The fall hadn't knocked the air from his lungs, but nonetheless, he found it hard to breathe with her lying on his chest.

"Are you okay?" There was that breathy whisper again, uncertain, a bit nervous. And unless he missed his guess, tinged with an acute awareness of him as a man.

"Okay," he replied, hating for this moment to end.

"Please take your seats," a flight attendant said sharply as she rushed over. "And buckle yourselves in."

"Let me help you up," Charlize offered, rising to her feet with amazing agility and grace for a woman wearing three-inch heels and a mean pair of stockings.

He almost laughed at the notion of a slender branch like her helping a tree trunk like himself to his feet. But he liked the idea of touching her again, so he put out his hand, which dwarfed hers, and allowed her to tug him.

Quinn pushed against the floor of the plane, and his own momentum brought him to a standing position. The top of her sleek head only came to his armpit. Her hip was level with his upper thigh. She seemed as perfect and delicate as the first butterfly of spring.

Without a doubt she was the most exquisite woman he'd ever met. Her straight blond hair was cut in a polished style and appeared as finely spun as silk. Her complexion was flawless, except for a small scar below her right earlobe. He had an almost overpowering urge to explore that scar with the tip of his tongue.

How he wanted to say something more to her, to do

something more with her, but the frowning flight attendant was clucking her tongue and waving at them to take their seats. Charlize scooted past him, her breasts lightly brushing his upper arm, causing a brushfire to leap up his nerve endings, and made her way to her seat.

Kay was practically panting as she clicked the seat belt in place around her waist. Her heart pounded, blood suffused her skin. She couldn't believe what had just happened and her body's heated response to a stranger. Touching him had been far more electric, far more satisfying than her wildest imaginings.

She didn't look up, because she knew he was still standing there staring at her as if he'd been struck with a bolt from the blue. What was the matter with him? Didn't they have women wherever it was he was from?

"You sure you're all right?" He squatted in the aisle beside Kay, defying the angry flight attendant, who looked as if she wanted to tie him into his seat but was too quelled by his size to approach.

"I'm fine, don't worry about me. Please, for your own safety, sit down."

"If you need me, I'm right behind you." He touched her wrist with his massive paw, and her blood slipped through her veins like quicksilver. Intense. So intense. If she closed her eyes, she could see the two of them in a forest. Walking. Alone. On a bed of soft, mossy ground. The sunlight flitting through the trees.

Stop it, stop it, stop it. Don't you dare go into another sexual fantasy, Kathryn Victoria Freemont!

She raised her hand to her face. The hand that had been wrapped in his. She smelled of him. Robust, masculine. Like pine needles, wilderness and soap. A shiver she could not suppress overtook her body. She could easily imagine him back there in his seat watching her with eagle eyes.

What was it about this man that so stirred her blood? What was it that made her feel giddy and girlish and oh-so-happy to be alive?

Kay was kidding herself, and she knew it. Just because he made her feel desirable didn't mean she was licensed to jump his bones. She didn't even know the guy's name. What he made her feel was simply a reflection of her wishful thinking. She wanted rescuing from her life, and he was a convenient escapist illusion.

Because lately, nothing in her current experiences seemed to satisfy her. Not her relationship with her parents, who were pressuring her to marry Lloyd and produce an heir. Certainly not her romance with Lloyd, if you could even call what they had a romance.

Lloyd had proposed to her by e-mail two days ago in a manner as romantic as a root canal. His exact message had been "Your father says he'll make me partner if we're married by the end of the summer, guess it's time to do the deed."

Whoopee! Sweep a girl right off her feet, why don't you?

She'd ignored Lloyd's e-mail, pretending she hadn't yet seen the missive, because she wasn't ready to deal with it, and surprise, surprise, he hadn't even called her in Chicago to see why she hadn't responded.

And even her job as a reporter for *Metropolitan* magazine no longer fulfilled her as it once had.

"What happened to you?" she whispered to herself, grateful no one was seated next to her. "In college, you dreamed of writing novels and having adventures and taking a lover that was as kind and considerate and understanding as he was good in bed. Where did that girl go?''

It seemed her entire youth had been spent trying to please Mommy and Daddy and striving to be the perfect Freemont. Her one tiny insurrection had been insisting on studying journalism rather than art history, as her mother had wished.

''Lloyd Post comes from blueblood stock, dear, just like you,'' her mother had told her when she called the day before to see if Kay had gotten Lloyd's e-mailed proposal. Apparently Lloyd had already discussed it with her parents. Would have been nice if he'd talked things over with her first. ''Give his proposition some serious thought. You could do worse than marrying him.''

Hmm, what was worse than binding yourself for life to a man who virtually ignored you for weeks on end? What was worse than until death do you part with a man who didn't even care where your G-spot was located? What was worse than spending the next forty years beside a guy with whom you had absolutely nothing in common other than the fact you were both filthy rich with impeccable pedigrees?

Let's see, what was worse than marrying Lloyd Post?

Well, owing money to the Mafia had to be a bummer. Being stranded in the desert with no water wasn't cool. Having oral surgery wasn't a blast. So yes, Mommy, you're absolutely right. There are worse things than marrying Lloyd.

But there were so many better things, too.

Like taking that rugged woodsman to bed?

She tried to picture what would happen if she was to walk into her parents house on Paul Bunyon's arm and announce they were engaged. Laughable! Even she, of the overactive imagination, could not conceive of such an event.

Helplessly she found her head drawn to the right, her eyes peeping surreptitiously over her shoulder.

And there he was, just as she knew he'd be. Staring at her and not a bit ashamed of his unabashed appreciation.

He was pure testosterone in a huge package that proclaimed, "I'll never let any harm come to you." It was a heady promise. Between his protective attitude and his raw animal magnetism, the man oozed an essential sexiness that called to something wild within her. Like a wolf to his mate. Something primal and elemental she hadn't known she possessed until now.

She deserved to be happy. She deserved to be sexually satisfied, and she deserved far better than settling for Lloyd Post. In reality she knew Paul Bunyon did not figure into her future, but regardless, meeting him at this juncture had changed her. It was time she stood up to her parents and started living her own life. It was past time she found out what she'd been missing.

QUINN PLANNED to waylay her in the jetway, help her with her luggage, hail her a taxi, get her phone number and ask her out to dinner. In fact, he was so excited about the idea that he'd kept shifting restlessly in his seat, unable to think of anything else.

But when the plane landed at JFK, she leaped from her seat the minute the flight attendants opened the door. Quinn got up to follow her, but an elderly lady sitting across the aisle asked him to retrieve her carry-on bag from the overhead bin. What else could he do?

By the time he made his way into the terminal, Charlize had vanished as if she'd never existed.

He looked left, then right, but the crowd had swallowed her. How could she have disappeared so quickly?

Damn!

He hadn't mistaken her interest in him, no matter how cool she liked to play it. The attraction had been instant and physical. No denying her raspy breathing when he'd held her in his arms, no hiding her aroused nipples. She'd wanted him, all right.

So why had she run away?

Maybe she was married, the thought occurred to him, but he didn't recall seeing a ring on that delicate third finger of her left hand.

Ah, well. Quinn wasn't the sort to cry over spilt milk. He took a deep breath and headed for the baggage claim. Nothing to be done about it now. He tried to push her from his thoughts.

But despite his best intentions, he couldn't help feeling he'd lost out on something pretty darn terrific.

"KAY, COME HERE, you've got to see this." Her editor, Judy Nessler, stood in the doorway of Kay's office on Monday morning, grinning from ear to ear and crooking a bejeweled finger at her.

Kay frowned and glanced up from the piece she was working on about finding love on the Internet. She'd gone to Chicago to interview a couple who'd met in an online chat room, and she had her notes spread out on the desk around her. Included in the pile were copies of the spicy messages the couple had posted to each other during their courtship. Reading the sizzling missives had her feeling oddly cranky.

"What is it, Judy?"

"Ask me no questions and I'll tell you no lies."

She wasn't in the mood for Judy's guessing games. It had been almost twenty-four hours since her plane ride with Paul Bunyon, but she couldn't seem to stop spinning fantasies about him. How could the thought of one man make her ache so badly?

Nor had she been able to locate Lloyd in order to pin him down for a dinner date to discuss his marriage proposal in person, and he hadn't yet returned the call she had left on his answering machine.

"I'm in the middle of something," Kay said.

"Just come with me."

Sighing, Kay pushed away from her desk and followed Judy down the corridor to the advertising department. As usual, the room was abuzz with activity. But atypically, all the activity seemed concentrated in the middle of room. Centered, in fact, around a skyscraper-size man who had his back to them.

A man clad in red flannel and blue denim. His head was cocked to one side and he was laughing at something one of the blushing assistants had said. Kay's pulse momentarily stuttered to a stop. She raised a hand to her throat.

No. It couldn't be.

Judy leaned in close and whispered, "You don't see guys like him traipsing up Fifth Avenue every day of the week."

Please, don't let it be Paul Bunyon, Kay prayed, but in her heart she knew.

Judy took her by the elbow and dragged her across the room like a reluctant puppy on a leash.

"Quinn," Judy said. "I'd like you to meet Kay Freemont, one of our top writers."

Slowly he pivoted on one booted heel, an insouciant gleam in his eye. Then recognition hit. His brows sprung up on his forehead and the grin went from free and easy to downright seductive.

It was Paul Bunyon! What an awful coincidence.

Of all the magazine offices in Manhattan, he had to walk into mine.

Why was he here? Was this some kind of a sign, him showing up so unexpectedly? Was the universe trying to tell her something?

"Kay, this is Quinn Scofield from Bear Creek, Alaska."

She stared at him.

He stared back at her.

Neither of them spoke.

The air around them seemed to vibrate with heat and energy and overpowering awareness.

Quinn. From Alaska. The Mighty Quinn. She should have known he would have a macho moniker. The name fit him like the mackinaw he wore.

Puzzled, Judy watched them watching each other. "Have you two already been introduced?"

"Actually, no." Quinn didn't even wait for Kay to offer her hand. He simply took it, and her blood puddled like melted butter in the pit of her stomach. "I'm very honored to make the acquaintance of such a lovely lady."

Pul-leeze. Enough with the flattery. I just saw you flirting with that assistant.

And yet, a small frisson of pleasure spiraled through her body and lodged with stunning acuity in her most feminine parts. If anything, her attraction to him was even stronger than it had been the day before.

Scary.

When Kay finally tore her gaze from his face, she realized that all the single women—and more than a few of the married ones—in the room were looking at her as if she'd snatched a prized morsel of filet mignon from their mouths.

"Quinn's come to New York looking for a wife," Judy said.

A wife? Kay took a step backward.

She jerked a quick glance in Quinn's direction and saw he was observing her reaction to Judy's news. Oh, boy, and here she'd been dreaming of having a red-hot fling with him. Well, certainly not now!

She'd just about decided to give old Lloyd the heave-ho and to tell her parents she was tired of living her life to suit them. She was ready to stretch her sexual wings and fly. She was not getting involved with a man who was looking for a commitment. No way. No matter how sexy he might be.

"He wants to place this full-page color ad with us." Judy took the advertising copy from an assistant and handed it to Kay.

Full-page color-ad space in *Metropolitan* magazine didn't come cheap.

"The four of us pitched in," Quinn said, as if reading Kay's mind. "The bachelors of Bear Creek."

"Doesn't that have a great ring to it?" Judy's eyes glistened. Clearly she was enamored of Quinn, his buddies and their ad.

Kay stared down at the photograph in her hand and sucked in her breath. Pictured were four of the most gorgeous men she'd ever laid eyes on, one of them Quinn. They looked sexier and far more masculine than anything Madison Avenue could have dreamed up. The men wore blue jeans, devilish grins and nothing else, their hunky, well-muscled bare chests on prominent display.

In the photo Quinn was lounging on one end of a black leather couch. He was bigger than she'd even imagined, with the buffest biceps on the planet. Draped across the other side of the couch was a coal-haired, blue-eyed Adonis with a dreamy, angelic air about him. On the floor, perched atop a bearskin rug, sat a dishy blond man with more charisma than a movie star, and another dark-eyed man with a lantern jaw and deep-set brown eyes. All four men were looking straight into the camera as if staring into the eyes of a beautiful woman.

Her gaze went from the one-dimensional, bare-chested Quinn to the fully three-dimensional Quinn standing beside her, and she gulped.

"That's Caleb Greenleaf," he said, leaning over her shoulder and pointing to the Adonis. "He's a naturalist for the state of Alaska. And that's Jake Gerard and Mack McCaulley. Jake runs the local bed-and-breakfast, and Mack's a bush pilot."

But Kay wasn't thinking about Caleb or Jake or Mack, no matter how good-looking they were. She was completely and totally distracted by Quinn's warm breath fanning the hairs on the nape of her neck.

Her gut tripped. She inhaled sharply and caught the arresting scent of his subtle aftershave and heated male flesh. That delicious smell sent her senses reeling.

Shaking her head to dispel the sultry cocoon Quinn had woven around her, Kay returned her attention to the glossy paper in her hand. Beneath the photograph of the four very eligible bachelors was the provocative caption: *Wild Women Wanted!*

"Do you have what it takes to be a wilderness wife?" was the first line of copy.

For absolutely no reason at all, Kay's heart fluttered. That line shouldn't have titillated her. She definitely did not have what it took to be a wilderness wife. She considered eating fast food roughing it. She had a low tolerance for cold weather, and she was scared to death of creatures like wolves and moose and bears.

Of course, if you had a man like Quinn to protect you from the cold and the critters, it might make Alaska a little more palatable. Still, a life without four-star restaurants, Broadway shows and department stores was too dismal to consider.

"I love this whole idea," Judy was chattering to Quinn. "Sexy bachelors forced to advertise in the lower forty-eight states to find wives. It's romantic. It's enchanting. It's a modern-day fairy tale. Our readers will eat it up. In fact, I'd like to run a feature article on the four of you."

"We could hold a contest," Kay volunteered, her marketing instincts kicking in, despite the fact that she really wanted nothing more to do with this particular bachelor and his wife hunt. "In thirty words or less tell us why you'd like to win a free trip to Bear Creek, Alaska. That sort of thing."

"Fabulous!" Judy enthused, and patted Kay's cheek. "You're such a dynamo. I knew you'd have something valuable to say. I love the idea. Simply love it. Then we can do a follow-up story on the contest winner. And who knows, if any of the guys find a wife as a direct result of the ad, we can do follow-up articles all through the year. I'll have to run this by Hal first, but I know he's going to adore it, too."

Kay shrugged, playing it cool as always. Freemonts never acted too eager.

"So what do you say, Kay? Ready to pack your bags and spend a couple of weeks in Alaska?" Judy asked.

"What?" She shook her head, thrown off by Judy's question. "Me go to Alaska?"

"Well," Quinn said, "late February probably isn't the best time of year to visit. When I left home, it was ten below."

"No kidding?" Judy whistled. "That is cold. But if we want the article to run with your ad in our June issue, then there's no time to waste. Kay can do it. She's pretty intrepid, aren't you, darling?"

Ten degrees below zero! Kay shivered at the very idea. "Are you nuts?"

"Come on, where's your spirit of adventure?" Judy goaded her. "Besides, it's perfect for the article. You can tell the readers firsthand that being an Alaskan wife is not for the faint of heart. Marriage-minded, handsome, successful bachelors do not come without some kind of price tag."

Kay shook her head. She was not going to Alaska—it would give Quinn the wrong idea. He might start thinking she was interested in becoming his bride. Besides, she had to settle things with Lloyd. "I'm sorry, I can't commit to this project right now—I've got too much on my plate. Why don't you ask Carol? I'm sure she'd love to go."

Was it her imagination, or did Quinn look disappointed? The notion that he wanted her to come to Alaska did strange things to Kay's insides.

"Don't give me your answer yet," Judy said. "I

still have to talk to Hal. Then you can make up your mind. How's that sound?''

''All right, but don't tell Hal that I've agreed to sign on yet.''

''Understood. Now why don't you take Quinn to lunch? In fact, take the rest of the afternoon off. Show him New York. Since you're practically engaged, I know you won't be a threat to his bachelorhood and snatch him off the market before the ad even has a chance to run.''

3

PRACTICALLY ENGAGED.

So that explained why she'd fled from the airplane before he'd had a chance to ask her name. She'd been as attracted to him as he was to her, and very clearly disturbed by that attraction because she was in a serious, committed relationship.

Damn.

And he'd come to New York in person, rather than handling the details of placing the ad over the phone or through the mail, not only because he was considering purchasing new wilderness gear from a sporting goods outfit run by an old friend, but because he'd secretly hoped to have one last sexual adventure before seriously beginning his wife search.

With all his heart and soul, Quinn believed in monogamy. His parents, who'd had a solid, loving marriage for forty years and still counting, provided him with a blueprint. Once he made a commitment to a woman, he'd be hers for life. But until he found her, well, he was a red-blooded male, after all. He had physical needs. Needs that were growing stronger by the minute.

He'd known from the moment he'd watched Kay Freemont board the plane that he wanted her, and then to find her working in the office of *Metropolitan* magazine—unbelievable! He'd taken it as a positive sign that she was supposed to be his passionate last fling. But now, to discover that she was practically engaged. Where did that leave him? He wasn't the sort of guy who came between a woman and her almost fiancé.

Then again, what the hell did "practically engaged" mean, anyway? Quinn ran a hand through his hair. Where he came from, either you were engaged or you weren't. Maybe it was a New York thing.

"Well." Kay nodded and looked rather uncomfortable with the assignment of baby-sitting him for the rest of the afternoon. "Well."

Had her boss's edict to wine and dine him left her at a loss for words? Or was it something more? Was it meeting him again?

Dream on, Scofield.

And yet, that was exactly what he wanted to do. Dream on and on and on of taking her to bed. Seeing her in her work environment, amid people who obviously admired and respected her, looking so professional and self-possessed in that short-skirted purple business suit made him crave her even more. Did she have any earthly idea what those magnificent legs of hers did to a man? Women who were practically engaged and possessed legs like Thoroughbreds should not be allowed to wear skirts like that! There oughtta be a law.

Damn, but the woman blew him away! Her cocoa-brown eyes simmered with a suppressed sexuality that begged to be brought to a boil. When he had turned and spied her beside Judy Nessler, adrenaline walloped him in the gut.

Now, simply standing here next to her, inhaling her scent—a fetching combination of vanilla ice cream and sharply scented cinnamon sticks—his body came alive.

To the point where he wished for a bucket of ice cubes to chill his throbbing member.

"Your cologne smells nice. What's it called?"

"White Heat."

He angled her a glance. "White Heat, huh? It suits you."

"Pardon?"

He could tell by the way she pursed her lips that he'd unnerved her. "You're like white heat. You've got this cool, outer demeanor, but inside, there's a deep, smoldering flame."

She gulped. He watched her struggle to control her features. She hated giving away her thoughts, he realized, and she'd mastered the art of suppressing her emotions.

How he longed to unsuppress her. To teach her how to open up and say exactly what was on her mind.

"Uh, let me get my bag and coat and change my shoes." She gestured in the direction of what he supposed was her office. "And we can grab some lunch."

She dashed away, leaving him to rein in his hormones, and returned a few minutes later wearing a black leather coat with an oversize purse thrown over her shoulder and a pair of Nikes on her feet. He almost laughed at the sight of her in that glamorous business suit and shod in running shoes, but once they were out on the street, he noticed a lot of the women similarly dressed. He commented on it.

"Try walking twelve blocks in high heels. You'd carry a spare pair of sneakers in your bag, too."

"We don't even have blocks in Bear Creek." He grinned.

She gave him a strange look as if he was speaking Mandarin. And it struck him then how different their lives were. He could survive alone in the Alaskan wilderness for weeks if necessary, but in New York City, he feared being unable to survive something as simple as crossing the street. He couldn't understand how people lived here day in and day out. The pollution, the noise, the crowds. Eventually it had to drive you out of your mind.

Kay stepped off the curb and raised her hand. A taxi glided to a stop at their feet.

How'd she do that? he marveled. When he'd tried to get a taxi to carry him to the magazine office, he'd been ignored. Was he so obviously an out-of-towner? Or did she know some taxi-halting secrets? Then again, if he was a cab driver, he would willingly risk whiplash to jam on the brakes for those legs.

Quinn moved to open the taxi door for her. Kay gave him an odd look, then scooted across the back seat of the cab to make room for him.

"You don't have to do the he-man routine with me."

"What?" He stared at her, puzzled.

Kay could tell he had no clue what she was talking about. "You know. First the door to the building, now the cab. I can open my own doors, you know."

"Oh. Sorry. I didn't mean to offend. It's just habit. My mother drilled good manners into my head. I'll try to stop if you want."

"No. Please forget I mentioned it."

She immediately felt badly for saying anything. She had to remember he was an Alaskan and obviously rather old-fashioned. He probably carried a clean hankie in his shirt pocket at all times in case some damsel burst into tears. Plus, she was accustomed to Lloyd only opening doors for her when they were around other people. Putting on a show to impress his business associates.

Honestly, she'd never met anyone quite like Quinn.

Kay took him to a Cuban restaurant that served to-die-for mahi-mahi with mango chutney, black beans, rice and fried plantains. And as she suspected, he told her that he'd never tasted anything like this exotic fare as the food disappeared from his plate.

He also told her stories about Alaska. About his loyal friends and loving family. Then he asked her questions about New York. He spoke with such open animation, she was helplessly drawn to his enthusiasm. He didn't play games, he didn't pull punches. Her parents would probably have thought him too loud and too eager, but she found his down-to-earth candor refreshing.

"So tell me," he said after he'd polished off the last crumb of key lime pie. "How long have you been 'practically' engaged."

She could tell by the way he said "practically" that he found the notion ridiculous. "Lloyd and I have been dating four years."

"Your guy's commitment-phobic, huh? Hasn't gotten around to popping the question, but you're expecting him to?"

"No, that's not it. I mean, well, actually, he did ask me to marry him a few days ago."

"So you are engaged." His tone was flat. She saw disappointment in his eyes.

"No."

"You turned him down?" Hope flared fresh in his face, and the sight of his renewed optimism confused her.

"No."

He frowned. "I don't understand. You told him you'd think about it?"

"It didn't happen that way. Listen, I really don't feel comfortable discussing my personal life with you."

"Okay." He gave an easy shrug, but she could tell by the look in his eyes that he wanted to dig deeper. What she didn't know was why, but she certainly wasn't going to open up and spill her guts to a stranger.

Not even her closest friends knew what was in her heart. She'd been taught by her father, the cutthroat businessman, that the more people knew about you, the more they could use against you. Once, when she was a little girl, her father took her to work with him. When his secretary asked her if she'd rather be playing in the park, instead of touring a stuffy old building, Kay had responded with an enthusiastic yes. Her father then jerked her into his office and lectured her until her ears burned about expressing her true feelings to underlings. She never forgot that lesson.

Quinn cleared his throat. The waiter refilled their coffee cups.

"I'm sorry about what I said," Kay said. "That sounded bitchy."

"No need to apologize. You're right. It's none of my business. It's just that if I was dating a woman like you, I wouldn't have waited four years to ask you to marry me."

"Which raises the question, if you're not commitment-phobic yourself, how come you've stayed single so long?"

"Not a lot of women to choose from in Bear Creek. And most of the tourists that come to town are looking for a summer fling. And who's to say I've never been married?''

''Have you?'' Kay lifted an eyebrow. Although she hated answering personal questions herself, she had no compunction against asking them. Enjoyed it, in fact. Perhaps that's what attracted her to journalism. The opportunity to discover the intimate details of others' lives without revealing any information about her own.

''Came close once.''

''What happened?''

''Now I'm the one who's uncomfortable discussing my private life.''

''Whoever writes the feature article on you is going to want to know the answer to these questions.''

''Then I'll save the interview for that reporter.''

Silence.

''So in general, what qualities do you look for in a woman?'' She spoke lightly, but every cell in her body stood at attention as she waited for his answer.

''I don't really want a career woman. I know it sounds old-fashioned, but I see myself with a woman who's mainly interested in making a home. I want kids. And I like the idea of providing for the woman in my life.''

''Oh, I see. The caveman mentality. Keep 'em barefoot and pregnant.''

''I don't mind if she wants to work,'' he expounded. ''But the children and I should be her priority. Just as she and the kids will be my top priority, not work, not a job. Family and friends. That's what counts. Don't look so disapproving. I'm being honest here.''

''I'm not disapproving. You're misconstruing my expression. Besides, does it matter what I think?''

The truth was, she'd been thinking that she'd never

heard a New York male express such a sentiment or, for that matter, even admit to wanting children. She found it oddly refreshing, even though one side of her wanted to argue that women could have both prosperous careers and happy, well-adjusted children if they learned how to juggle.

His gaze was on her face. He was running his index finger around and around the rim of his coffee mug in a slow, languid motion that made her feel dizzy with desire. "My ideal woman has to be tough. She's got to be hardy enough to brave winters in Alaska."

"What about beauty?"

"Beauty's good, but not really important. I mean, there's got to be sexual chemistry between us, but I'm not looking for perfection. On the contrary, I think a little sass, a little attitude spices things up."

"Really?"

"And even though I'm ready to settle down, I'm not willing to settle. When I get married, it'll be forever. Until then—" he grinned "—I'm up for whatever adventures come my way."

"Oh." At this, Kay took heart. Perhaps he might provide that illicit affair she was yearning for, after all.

"So what do you look for in a man, Kay Freemont?"

She shrugged. "I don't know."

"You don't know? Then how do you know if Mr. Practically Engaged is the right one for you?"

She winced. "Please, I—"

"Oh, right, no personal questions."

"How long are you in town?" She changed the subject and wondered what she was going to do with the information. Wondered why her heart was pounding.

"I fly out at seven-thirty on Wednesday morning.

Tomorrow I've got an all-day thing with my friend from Adventure Gear. I'm thinking of switching over to their climbing harnesses, and he's taking me on a climb upstate.''

''Ah.'' Her hopes plummeted. No time for a wild fling.

He reached across the table and lightly grazed her hand with the tips of his fingers. It shouldn't have been an erotic gesture, but it was.

''You could come to Alaska,'' he said, reading her thoughts as clearly as if they'd been etched on her face. His habit of expressing exactly what was on her mind was uncanny and, frankly, a little disturbing. ''Write that article for your editor. We could have a lot of fun together, you and I. Why not consider it?''

Astounded by the sensations that surged through her at his touch, she slipped her hand away. She never did answer his question.

After lunch he wanted to see the Empire State Building, so off they went. Quinn moved through the crowd like a redwood among matchsticks. On more than one occasion, she noticed women's heads turn as they shot him appreciative glances. She felt oddly jealous.

And strangely aroused.

More aroused, in fact, than she'd ever been.

While Quinn admired the view from the top of the Empire State Building, Kay admired Quinn.

She couldn't seem to draw her gaze from the ripple of muscle in his forearm where he'd rolled back the sleeves of his mackinaw. It was as if he knew how much she loved sexy forearms and was simply taunting her with a view of his.

She studied his strong profile, raked her gaze down

his shoulders to his back before stopping to blatantly admire his delectable fanny so prominently displayed in snug-fitting blue jeans.

Raising a hand to her throat, she inhaled deeply, hauling in an unsteady breath. Quinn turned from the railing, a wide, boyish grin on his face. Kay smiled back.

"Wow. So many people. So many buildings. So many yellow-checkered cabs."

She nodded.

The wind gusted. Shivering, Kay used a pillar as a windbreak. She crossed her arms over her chest and danced from foot to foot.

"You're cold," he said, and she found it touching that he'd noticed. He stripped off his mackinaw.

"I can't take your jacket. It's freezing up here."

"Honey," he said, and she did not take offense at his easy endearment; rather, she found it kind of charming. "Where I'm from this would be considered a heat wave."

He stepped closer and settled his mackinaw around her shoulders, wrapping her as tenderly as a mother swaddles her baby.

"Thank you." Her voice emerged as a breathless whisper, and she realized they were the only people still on the observation deck. The cold had forced everyone else back inside.

"You're welcome."

Quinn peered down into her face and damned if little Miss Too-Cool-for-School didn't look nervous. The tip of her tongue darted out to wet her upper lip. Was her gesture an unconscious invitation to kiss her? God, he hoped so, because he wanted to do that more than anything in the world.

''Uh—'' she took a step backward ''—perhaps we should go now.''

''Why?'' His body was so very aware of hers. ''Are you frightened?''

She forced a laugh. ''Frightened of what? Heights?''

''Of this.''

Then, taking them both by surprise, he caught her upper arms in his hands, raised her to her toes and kissed her the way he'd been longing to kiss her since the moment he'd caught her in his arms on the airplane.

She yielded. Accepted him with ready acquiescence. Complied by parting her lips and letting him slip his tongue in deep to taste the honeyed, warm recesses of her mouth. Languidly his tongue glided against hers.

Lust, swifter, more vehement than anything he'd ever experienced, exploded inside him. And it was just a damned kiss.

His gut clenched hard. He could only imagine how his hardness sliding into her would feel, her slender arms entwined around his neck, her luscious tush cupped in his large palms.

He was not the kind of guy to sit idle on the sidelines. When he saw something he wanted, he went after it. But even he had never moved so fast or wanted anyone so strongly. He had no more control than a moose in rut. That's what this woman did to him.

Had he shocked her with his boldness? Had he indeed moved too quickly?

But no, she moaned softly and leaned into him. Quinn swallowed the sound, tilting her head back, threading his fingers through her hair. The softness of those silken strands was in sharp contrast to the hardness building inside him.

Incredible. Simply incredible.

He forgot that she was practically engaged. He forgot that he didn't steal other men's women. He forgot that she was out of his league. He forgot everything except how wonderful she felt, how good she tasted.

Kay held her breath, dazed and ashamed. Freemonts did not act like this! They didn't kiss strangers in public. They did not lose control. They did not succumb to wanton lust.

Good. Good. Good. Good.

She was no longer behaving like a Freemont, and it was liberating beyond description.

But what was she getting herself into?

Quinn, the Alaskan man who smelled of wilderness and tasted of mangoes and key lime pie, was giving her the most possessive kiss of her life. Branding her with his tongue, searing her with his passion.

She'd never experienced anything like it, certainly not with Lloyd or with that guy from college. Her heart did a triple backflip before taking on a frantic, galloping rhythm of thrill and response.

Up was down, down was up. Nothing made sense anymore, but it felt so right.

Was she indeed supposed to begin her journey of self-discovery with this man? Or was she kidding herself? Using his willingness as an excuse for acting out her long-hidden desires?

Splaying a hand on Quinn's chest, Kay thought to push him away, but instead, she let her hand rest there, feeling his heartbeat and marveling that it pounded as forcefully as her own.

Even through his flannel shirt, she could feel his muscled flesh. In spite of the cold, he felt blisteringly hot and wonderfully solid against her palm. She realized he was coiled as tense as a snake waiting to strike. The comparison alarmed her. Did she really believe he might be dangerous? What was she doing? She didn't know this man.

But that was rigid Freemont thinking, and more than anything she wanted to break free of the constraints of her old thought patterns. She wanted to stop berating herself, wanted to take some risks, inhale the danger, embrace the challenge, not fear it. She wanted to be fully alive. She wanted to replace fantasies with reality.

And Quinn was serving up huge helpings of reality on a silver platter.

Her knees were weak, her breath faint. How could one simple kiss do so many different things to her? Okay, it wasn't such a simple kiss. It was more like an implosion. His mouth caused her insides to topple and collapse in on themselves.

He tugged her close against his body, bringing her in startling contact with his rock-hard erection. One of his hands slipped underneath the hem of her leather coat to caress her behind.

Oh, my!

Everything she was feeling was so new, so exciting, so unbelievable, and precisely like one of her fantasies.

Quinn pulled his mouth from hers at last, his breath coming in jerky gasps. Her lips felt swollen and wet, her body both tight and liquid at the same time. He rubbed his cheek against hers, setting her on fire. She quivered and he pressed his lips to her ear.

"Woman," he whispered hoarsely, "I'm so turned on by you."

In that moment she experienced a unique and exhilarating power. She, cool, poised Kay Freemont, had made this mountain of a man lose control. She wanted more from him, and that was all there was to it.

What would your parents think? What about Lloyd? the nagging voice that made her do all the right things for all the wrong reasons piped up.

To hell with her parents. To hell with Lloyd. She'd been the dutiful daughter for twenty-seven years, and where had it gotten her?

An orgasmless career woman practically engaged to a man who did not even love her.

Marshaling her courage, Kay took Quinn's chin in her palm and looked him square in the eye. She'd never done anything like what she was about to do, and therein lay the thrill of it. She knew he would be a kind and gentle lover and maybe, just maybe, he would be the one to turn the key of her womanhood and lead her to new levels of physical joy.

His smoky-gray eyes met hers with a sheen of raw desire, and he did not look away. He didn't even blink. He stared into her eyes as if he could peer right into the depths of her soul.

"Yes?" he growled. This talent he had for anticipating her thoughts was downright spooky.

"Would you like to go back to my place?" she asked breathlessly.

Quinn couldn't believe his ears. "What? What did you say?"

She cleared her throat. "My place. You. Me. Now."

He shook his head, unable to comprehend his good fortune. "Are you sure?"

"No. I'm not sure of anything, except that for once in my well-ordered, well-behaved life I need to do something irresponsible and unpredictable and capricious. So let's go before I change my mind."

She grabbed his hand and started pulling him toward the elevators.

"Whoa, wait a minute." He dug in his heels and she couldn't budge him. "I don't want to be your biggest regret."

"Well, you should have thought of that before you kissed me."

"A kiss is one thing, Kay. Sex is something else entirely."

"That's what I'm counting on." Her voice was husky, her eyes heavy-lidded.

He shook his head again. What was the matter with him? This was his fantasy. So why was he putting on the brakes? Was he out of his ever-loving mind?

"Please."

Ah, this was killing him.

"You're a beautiful woman, and I want to make love to you so badly I can taste it. But I don't break up couples. And you're practically engaged."

"No. In fact, I was thinking I might break up with him."

"You don't love the guy?"

"I thought I did once. Or what passed for love. But lately I've come to understand that I don't even know what love is," she said. "My parents like Lloyd. They think we're great together. They're the ones pushing for this marriage."

"You let your parents tell you who to date?"

She took a deep breath, waved a dismissive hand. "Let's not talk about them. Let's not talk at all." She angled him a coy glance that almost brought him to his knees.

She looked so damned appealing standing there with the wind whipping his mackinaw around her shoulders, her golden hair falling across one cheek, her full lips pursed in fervid anticipation of his acquiescence, her hands cocked on her slender hips.

Much as he wanted to say yes, as much as he knew he'd be kicking himself tonight in his lonely hotel room, Quinn knew he had to turn her down.

He heaved in a heavy lungful of chilled air and shook his head. "I'm sorry, Kay, but I've got to say no."

4

OH GOD, SHE'D MADE a fool of herself. What had she been thinking? Freemont women did not throw themselves at perfect strangers, no matter how sexually appealing they were.

She tossed her head, averted her gaze.

"Don't be embarrassed. I'm flattered. Very flattered. You're one hell of a sexy woman."

His comment, meant to soothe, only served to fluster her more. Was she that transparent?

"I'm not embarrassed," she lied, and gave a casual shrug for good measure. "I asked—you weren't interested. I can handle rejection."

"Lady, you're wrong about that. I'm extremely interested. But you've got something to settle with that boyfriend of yours, and hopping into the sack with me won't solve your problems. I'm sorry." He reached out to take her hand, but she stepped back and shook her head.

Don't touch me. Please. If you do I'll crumble into your arms.

She held only the most tenuous control over her libido. These unstoppable, blazing-hot fantasies, combined with her lack of sexual release, had compelled her to do something she normally would never have done in a million years. And she was ashamed of herself. Best to get away from this man ASAP.

Especially since the hot tingling between her legs had not abated one whit since he'd kissed her.

"Look," she said with her usual crisp efficiency. "You're right. Maybe we should call it a day."

"Yeah," he murmured, and pushed the elevator button. "That'd probably be best."

Quinn gazed at her with such heated desire, with such greedy longing, Kay almost threw her arms around his neck and begged him to reconsider. But she didn't, of course. She was at her core a Freemont, after all.

She drew herself up straight. "Yes. Well, it's been an experience meeting you."

"Will I see you again? Are you coming to Alaska?"

She shook her head.

"I was afraid of that." He smiled wistfully. "Another time, another place."

Her heart hung suspended in her throat, and for some idiotic reason tears hovered behind her eyelids. Kay blinked. The elevator door dinged open.

"Come on," she said. "I'll hail you a cab."

She dropped him off at his hotel in Times Square, but asked the driver to linger a moment at the curb so she could watch him disappear through the revolving glass doors. She was too shaken to return to work. Besides, Judy had given her the rest of the afternoon off, and she'd be irritated to know Kay hadn't spent it squiring Quinn around town.

And besides, there was another matter that demanded her attention. She couldn't go forward with her life until she broke up with Lloyd. No more phone calls or e-mails. No more evading. This had to be face-to-face. She had a key to his place; she would go to his apartment and confront him. And if he wasn't home, she'd pack up the few things she kept stashed there and wait for him to return.

It was a plan. Taking action made her feel better. She gave the cabby Lloyd's address and leaned back.

Sighing, she wistfully trailed her fingers over the seat where Quinn had been sitting, the vinyl material warm from the heat of his body. She lowered her head, lifted her collar to her nose and breathed deeply of his scent, still clinging to her blouse.

What a masculine man.

Hair as thick and wavy as a Kansas cornfield. Eyes the color of a cold November sky. Warm, inviting lips that promised so much in that short but sizzling kiss they'd shared. Broad shoulders, honed waist, narrow hips.

Kay moaned under her breath, closed her eyes and pictured him with his shirt off.

He's splitting logs with an ax, and he's stripped bare to the waist. It's summer. Midday. Hot for Alaska.

She's watching him from a shelter of thick trees. The scent of pine fills her nostrils. Behind him in the distance rises snowcapped mountain peaks. He doesn't see her. She knows he's had trouble with hunters poaching his land, and he's not friendly toward secretive visitors spying on him from the trees.

She shouldn't be here, but she can't look away. She can't even move. Her eyes are transfixed on his exquisite, tanned torso.

His muscular biceps bunch as he swings the ax down in one long, smooth stroke.

Whack!

The ax strikes home with a metallic, hypnotic ring that echoes strangely in the still forest. Shivers of excitement run up her spine.

She licks her lips.

He pauses in his work. Rests one arm against the ax handle, swipes at his forehead with a blue bandanna pulled from the back pocket of his tight, denim jeans.

The sun glints seductively off the sweat beading his chest. A sultry heat settles low in her belly, then fans out like thick fingers, growing, clutching, pressing down on her, until every part of her body pulsates with awareness of his overt maleness.

She shifts her position, lifts her head higher, hoping for a better look. She startles a squirrel, which begins to chatter at her.

The woodsman jerks his head sharply in her direction.

"Who's there?" he calls out.

Heart racing, she jumps to her feet. She can't be discovered. No telling what he'll do to her if he finds her encroaching on his land.

"Show yourself," he demands.

She whirls around—must get away—and darts through the underbrush.

"Come back here, damn you."

She hears him crashing through the forest as he thunders after her, but she doesn't look behind her.

Something snags her blouse. The silky material splits wide open, exposing her bra. Her skirt, too, gets caught on something sharp. She hears the rip. Her clothes hang in tatters, flapping about her skin.

Thud, thud, thud.

He is coming.

Faster, run faster.

She tries, but it's as if her feet are encased in cement. She's moving in slow motion. She can hear his breathing as he gets closer.

Her hair streaks out behind her, and her legs churn through the thick carpet of pine needles. She zigzags around trees, leaps over downed logs like a doe fleeing a pursuing rutting buck. She's heading for the clearing and freedom. Her pulse is pounding, thumping, thrashing madly in her ears.

He's quick for a big man. So quick. And so very close now. She's not going to make it.

He tackles her. His arms go around her waist. He pulls her atop him as they fall together.

Then she's on her back and he's above her, pinning her arms to the earth with his knees. His breathing is raspy, ragged. There is an angry gleam in his smoldering eyes.

"Who are you?" he commands.

But she can't answer. She's so afraid. Her whole body trembles. What's he going to do to her?

"You were trespassing on my land."

She nods, fear and a strange feeling she's never had before pooling in her belly.

"You must be punished."

She squirms, trying to get free, but his knees hold her fast. She can't move. Can't get away. She is captured. His prisoner. Will he require her to be his love slave?

She catches her breath.

He grabs what's left of her blouse and rips it from her body. Her bra follows, exposing tender breasts. Her chest heaves as she exhales.

His hands, work-roughened and callused, are suddenly gentle as he massages her nipples. "I must teach you a lesson," he whispers. "You must learn never to spy."

She whimpers.

He leans over her, takes one nipple into his mouth, and she gasps. He plunders her with his tongue.

The pleasure is beyond description. She writhes beneath him wanting more punishment, more sweet torture....

"Lady—" the cabby's voice jerked her rudely back to reality "—that'll be seven-fifty."

She thrust a ten at him. Dazed and stuffy-headed from her interrupted fantasy, she stumbled out of the taxi.

The doorman greeted her with a smile, and Kay took the elevator to the penthouse and let herself into Lloyd's apartment. Emotionally exhausted, she dropped her purse on the table in the foyer and kicked off her shoes. This wasn't going to be easy.

That was when she heard the noises coming from the bedroom. She cocked her head, listening.

Giggles. Moans. Oohs. Ahhs. It sounded like someone having sex.

And not just any sex, but wild, uninhibited, swinging-from-the-chandelier monkey sex.

Bed springs squeaked. The headboard banged. *Ka-wham, ka-wham, ka-wham.*

"Oh, baby, yeah, you hot stud. Give me all you've got. That's it. That's right."

Kay froze. Who was in Lloyd's apartment having sex? His maid and her boyfriend?

She tiptoed down the hallway, her stocking feet gliding over the cool, terrazzo floor. She should be upset or offended on Lloyd's behalf; instead, she was weirdly curious. It sounded as if they were having a hell of a time.

His bedroom door stood slightly ajar. Kay pressed her body against the opposite wall of the hallway and angled her head around for a peek. She shouldn't be doing this, she knew, but she wanted to see how other people made love.

Clothing lay strewn across the carpet, a bra—that looked to be nothing short of a D cup—dangled over the shade of a thousand-dollar antique lamp.

"Faster! Harder!" the woman cried.

Kay inched closer, helpless to stop herself from watching. A man, garbed only in black socks, stood with his back to her, his arms supporting the woman bent over in front of him.

She recognized the man at once. No mistaking that bony behind. Shock jolted through her. It took a moment for her to react, but then Kay kicked the door open wide.

Startled, her wannabe-fiancé turned to gape at her, his body still embedded in the flesh of the buxom redhead in his arms.

"Kay!" he cried in a strangled voice. "What on earth are you doing here?"

TWO HOURS LATER Kay sat morosely in her darkened kitchen, staring at the crystal salt and pepper shakers that sandwiched a crystal napkin holder and slowly shredding a lace paper doily.

She felt empty inside. Empty, hollow and cold. She hugged herself tightly and clenched her jaw to stay the tears that threatened to roll down her cheeks if she dared let them.

It wasn't so much finding Lloyd with another woman that bothered her. No, what really upset Kay was the cruel words he'd hurled at her as he'd wriggled into his pants.

"I'm glad you caught me, Kay. I've hated sneaking

around behind your back. But you gave me no choice. Do you have any idea how frustrating it is being with a frigid woman?''

Frigid.

The word reverberated in her head. Was she really frigid? She'd suspected for many years she might be, but to have someone say it to her face caused her more pain than she could have imagined.

He blamed his cheating on her.

A sick sensation flipped over in Kay's stomach as she recalled the blissful expression on the red-haired woman's face. She had obviously been having a very good time with Lloyd. If he could satisfy that woman, then apparently his lousy technique wasn't the reason for Kay's lack of sexual arousal. It was true. She was frigid.

She dropped her head into her hands and softly began to cry. In that moment she felt so alone. All those years of struggling to be the perfect daughter, the perfect Freemont, had extracted an extravagant toll. Decades of watching her p's and q's, worrying about what other people thought and putting on a polished facade had resulted in a repressed personality.

In truth she didn't know who she was or what she wanted. If only she could activate her sexuality. If she could come alive in that area of her life, might it not be the gateway to freedom?

But how did she go about liberating her libido?

Then she thought of Quinn. With his heated kissing and his bedroom eyes, he'd obviously desired her. If anyone ever made her feel like a woman, it was him.

And she'd let him get away.

She stroked her lips with fingertips gone salty from her tears and wistfully recalled their kiss and the power of their connection. A shiver passed through her. Could Quinn light the fire in her that she feared did not even exist?

You're idealizing him, Kay. He's nothing but wish fulfillment. The inner, sensible voice that had guided her actions throughout her life spoke sternly.

Right.

Sighing, she raised her head and straightened her shoulders. Freemonts did not pine for the impossible.

At that moment her door buzzer went off.

Great. Just what she needed. Company. Kay trudged to the door and pressed the intercom. "Yes?"

"Dearest, it's Mommy. I'm coming up."

Oh, no! "Mother, I'm pretty busy."

"Sweetheart, you don't have to pretend with me. Lloyd has been to see your father. I know what happened between you two."

"Then you know I never want to see his two-timing ass again."

"Is that any way for a Freemont to talk?" her mother chided.

More Freemont guilt. "Come on up." She sighed again.

A few minutes later Honoria Freemont rushed into Kay's apartment with her hair freshly coiffed, smelling of expensive French perfume and wearing an impeccably tailored suit. Immediately she took both of Kay's hands in hers and led her to the couch.

"You look terrible, darling. Your eyes are red and puffy."

"I've been crying."

"Do you have any cucumbers? We could make a cold compress."

"Mother, I don't care if my eyes are swollen. I'm

in my own apartment. Don't worry, none of your friends are going to see me."

"Oh, you're in one of those moods."

"Yes, I do believe I am. Not two hours ago I caught my boyfriend in bed with another woman. Under the circumstances I'm entitled to be a little testy, don't you think?"

Her mother shifted, let go of Kay's hands. "You mustn't allow something like this to come between you and Lloyd."

Kay stared at her mother openmouthed. "What?" She wasn't sure she'd heard correctly. Was her mother suggesting she overlook Lloyd's blatant infidelity?

Gently Honoria reached out and pushed Kay's jaw up. "Lloyd is your father's right-hand man. He'd be lost without him."

"What's that got to do with me?"

Her mother would have frowned, but her recent Botox injection ruled that out. Instead, a disapproving look came into her eyes. "It's got everything to do with you, darling. One day Freemont Enterprises will belong to you."

"And I can't inherit without a man at my side?"

"Not just any man. You must have a husband who comes from the right stock. A man who knows how to navigate your world. A man of good breeding."

"Oh, from what I witnessed this afternoon, Lloyd's good at breeding, all right." Kay crossed her arms and glared. How could her own mother side with her father and Lloyd in this matter?

"Don't be crude. It's unbecoming of a Freemont."

If her mother said one more word about being a good Freemont, Kay was going to scream. She rubbed her pounding temples.

"I'm not saying what Lloyd did was right," Honoria went on, "but he's very sorry. He's already apologized to your father, and he desperately wants to apologize to you, but he's afraid you won't speak to him."

"He's right. I never want to see him again."

"You're making a grave mistake. Lloyd comes from a long and illustrious bloodline."

"I'm not a racehorse, Mother."

"You're going to be seeing him at every social function. You know he's got opera-season tickets right next to our box. There's no way to avoid him."

"So I'll stop attending social functions and, news flash, I hate opera."

"You can't avoid him forever."

"Then I'll ignore him."

"Darling, you're old enough to understand this." Her mother patted her knee. "There're certain things a woman must put up with in a marriage. Any marriage. Be it good, bad or indifferent."

"And infidelity is one of those things?"

She simply couldn't believe her mother was saying this to her. Then again, what did she expect? Her mother had chosen to look the other way whenever Kay's father came home with lipstick on his collar or took late-night telephone calls in his den or went on "business" trips several times a month. Well, not her! She'd be damned if she'd live that way. No amount of money or social status was worth that kind of misery.

Kay got to her feet. "Mother, I think it's time for you to go."

Honoria looked startled. "Excuse me?"

"I'm not going to discuss Lloyd Post. I'm not going

to marry a man who cheats on me. You might have been willing to settle for a marriage in name only, but not me.''

Her mother looked as if she'd been slapped across the face with a broom. ''Kathryn Victoria Freemont, I will not allow you to speak that way to me.''

''Then if you don't want to hear what I have to say, there's the door.''

Flabbergasted, her mother picked up her purse. ''I'll talk to you later when you've come to your senses.''

''Don't hold your breath,'' Kay muttered, and locked the door behind Honoria, then collapsed onto the tiled floor and drew her knees to her chest. She rocked back and forth in a vain attempt to comfort herself the way she had as a little girl on Nanny's night off.

Oh, God, she had to get out of the city. Away from Lloyd's humiliating behavior, away from her father's chiding disapproval, away from her mother's terrible advice.

When had her life become such a mess?

From the outside, strangers might be envious of her. She had a plum job at the most successful women's magazine in the country. She had lots of money, got invited to all the right parties. She was thin and young and blond.

But others had no idea what it was like to be Kay Freemont. She was miserable to the core and hadn't a clue how to salvage herself. All her life she'd had this bizarre sensation of being on the inside looking out. While in the midst of prestige, money and privilege, she dreamed of being like other kids, wearing clothes off the rack, cheap sunglasses and colorful, rubber flip-flops.

She'd longed to do simple things like eat cotton candy or ride on a carnival Ferris wheel or lie on her back in the grass and stare up at a canopy of stars.

Instead, she'd been escorted to the planetarium and the museum by bodyguards. She'd been forced to attend boring parties and was kept isolated from ordinary people.

She was sick of it. And she wanted out.

For the longest time she had experienced no passion, no fire, no zest for life. That is, until yesterday when she had met Quinn Scofield.

Something about the man—be it his ruggedly sexy appearance, his independent nature, his engaging smile—stirred dormant emotions deep inside her. For the first time in years she felt excited.

The man was real; he didn't hide behind a facade. He was honest; he spoke what was on his mind, consequences be damned. He had true friends, not leeches who sucked up to him for his power and money. And he had family who loved him for who he was. In other words, he was everything she was not.

Go to Alaska. Write the feature article. Get away. Spend some time with Quinn. Tell him you've broken things off with Lloyd. Find yourself. Find your sexuality. Come home a new woman.

It sounded so good.

Determined, Kay crossed to the telephone in the alcove, picked up the receiver and called Judy to tell her she was taking the assignment. She was going north to Alaska.

5

KAY FREEMONT was coming to Bear Creek. Quinn still couldn't quite get his head around the notion. To think, in less than an hour, that cool, sleek beauty would be strolling the streets of his hometown.

The notion was enough to give a man the shakes. He wasn't quite prepared for the reality of her visit, and yet he didn't feel as if he could wait another second, much less sixty minutes or more.

She had already arrived in Anchorage, and Mack had flown out to retrieve her. Quinn could scarcely sit still. He had reserved the best room for her at Jake's B&B and arranged for her to borrow his parents' extra vehicle. Since his mother had slipped on ice and broken her right ankle the week before, she wouldn't need the old Wagoneer, anyway. He'd stocked his refrigerator with supplies, planning to cook a few meals for her. Quinn was proud of his culinary abilities and couldn't wait to show off for her.

And he was hoping against hope that his wildest dreams might come true and they could finish what they started in New York City. He had stopped by Leonard Long Bear's sundries store and picked up a box of condoms, a bottle of massage oil and edible body paints. Bear Creek might be small but because of the cruise ship trade, Long Bear's had to be prepared for every kind of request. Especially those of a confidential nature.

Unfortunately Quinn's private business hadn't remained private for long. By lunchtime at least half a dozen townspeople had kidded him about the naughty thoughts running through his mind.

Fine. Let them talk. He wasn't ashamed of his sexuality. Particularly since he hadn't had sex in more than eighteen months.

He hoped he could keep himself under control. He wanted to please Kay as much as he wanted to be pleasured. That kiss they'd shared atop the Empire State Building told him she was as hungry for physical love as he.

He couldn't wait to taste those lips again, to caress her soft flesh, to run his fingers through her silky hair. For the past week, ever since Judy Nessler had called and told him Kay was on her way, he'd been unable to consider anything else. Although he couldn't help but wonder if she was still "practically engaged" or if she had broken things off with her boyfriend.

Just thinking about Kay stirred him, and he had to breathe deeply and think of ice hockey in order to calm down.

Finally, finally, he heard the sound of Mack's bush plane glide to a stop in the inlet. Bundled in his parka, he threw open his front door and hurried down the walkway that was already covered with a light dusting of fresh flakes, even though he'd shoveled it earlier.

The first of March was an awful time to visit Bear Creek. They wouldn't be able to do much beyond sit by the fire. Kay certainly didn't seem the type to snowshoe or snowmobile or ice-skate. He couldn't see her sitting in the bleachers wrapped in thermal blankets at his hockey games. Ah, but he could visualize her curled up in his bed.

By the time he reached the dock, Mack had already helped her from the plane. Quinn took one look at her and his heart flipped.

She smiled in that cool, controlled way of hers. ''Hello, Quinn.''

He'd been nervous, not knowing exactly how to proceed, but in that moment instinct took over. He swung her into his arms, lifted her off her feet and hugged her to his chest.

''Welcome to Bear Creek, Kay,'' he whispered in her ear. ''I'm so glad you decided to come.''

''Thank you.'' She stiffened in his arms and he realized that his easy informality made her uncomfortable.

He sat her gently on the ground, wanting to respect her need for distance, and surveyed her with hungry eyes. She looked good, if somewhat out of place, in her virgin-white ski outfit and snowboots. It was probably the only cold-weather gear she owned.

Feeling self-conscious before Quinn's intense perusal, Kay adjusted the knit cap she wore. She loved the way he'd swung her into his arms but she had a hard time relaxing and enjoying his ebullience.

Mack, the bush pilot, busied himself with tying down the plane and pretending he wasn't eavesdropping on their conversation. She had enjoyed talking to the down-to-earth man on the flight over, and she'd been unable to stop herself from pumping him for information on Quinn. Now she feared Mack knew exactly how much she liked Quinn. For a woman who'd spent her life hiding her feelings from the world, this was a disconcerting prospect.

"Well," she said. "Well."

Her heart was galloping a mile a minute. On the long flight to Alaska she had decided once and for all to use that sexy underwear she had stuffed into her suitcase and seduce this bear of a man. One way or the other, she was bound and determined to prove Lloyd wrong. She was not frigid.

But now that she was here, staring into Quinn's mesmerizing gray eyes, an odd sensation of anticipation, excitement and fear gripped her. Her brain short-circuited, issuing two simultaneous but opposing commands.

Run for your life! Get out while you can!

Strap your arms around him and never let go!

Oh, God, she wanted him so badly. Maybe too much. But did she have the guts to go through with this? Were her expectations of this chemistry between them unrealistic?

He looked impressive in his fur-lined parka and all-weather boots. A rugged man's man who needed no fancy gym to keep in shape. Life in the Alaskan wilderness was his personal trainer.

Another twinge of anticipation. This time low in her anatomy. Heavens above, she was scared and thrilled.

You don't have to do anything you don't want to do, she reminded herself. *After all, you're here to write an article. Focus on that. Forget the other for now.*

That admonition and a deep breath of frosty winter air calmed her nerves.

Quinn held out his gloved hand to her. Tentatively she accepted it and allowed him to lead her cautiously up the snow-dazzled sidewalk to his rustic log cabin, which was perched on a small hill just above the shoreline.

"Come inside." He ushered her over the threshold, stopping long enough to stomp the snow off his boots on the welcome mat. Kay followed suit.

"Let me hang up your coat."

Kay started to pull down the zipper, but her fingers, even through her leather gloves, were so cold that she fumbled.

"Allow me." He reached for the zipper. Their hands brushed briefly. They both tried to ignore the contact. She glanced at the moose head mounted over the mantel, while he kept his eyes trained to the floor.

Rubbing her palms together, she gazed around the cabin. It was obvious he'd tidied up. The room smelled of pine cleaner and air freshener. The floor was hardwood and covered with a thick, braided rug. Hockey trophies were displayed in a glass case. In one corner sat a massive fireplace, in the other, a big-screen television with satellite hookup. It was definitely a man's place, painted in dark, masculine colors and decorated with large, sturdy furniture. A brown leather couch, a bold scarlet recliner, a hand-carved rocking chair.

She shrugged out of her ski jacket and stripped off her ski pants. He took the garments from her and hung them on a rack by the door. When she felt confident enough to glance his way again, she apprehended his gaze in a leisurely stroll down her body. He took in her red cashmere sweater, her form-fitting black pants, her fluffy white after-ski boots.

Despite the fact that she was bundled up to the teeth, thermal underwear on from neck to ankles, the way he looked at her made Kay feel like Lady Godiva prancing through the town square in the altogether.

"Nice place," Kay said, trying her best to keep her tone upbeat and lighthearted, as if his perusal didn't affect her one bit. But her breathless, whispery voice gave her away.

"Here," he said eagerly, his voice no steadier than her own. "Stand by the fire, get warm. I'll make us some hot chocolate."

Hot chocolate? Had she stepped back in time to a simpler place, a simpler era? It was nice, very nice, but she felt out of place. A stranger in a strange land.

"That'd be great."

Then an appalling thought occurred to her. Was she supposed to lodge here with him? Not that she didn't want to stay with him. She just didn't want it assumed.

"Quinn?" She watched him move around the kitchen, which was separated from the living area by a waist-high counter. She heard the oven door open, saw him bend over and remove a cookie sheet.

The smell of chocolate-chip cookies filled the air. Handsome and he could cook. A deadly combo.

"Uh-huh." He deposited the cookie sheet on a cooling rack and glanced over at her. His hair had flopped boyishly over his forehead. For no good reason whatsoever her stomach did a backflip.

"Did you…am I…" She cleared her throat and tried again. "Where am I supposed to sleep?"

"At Jake's B&B a quarter mile up the road in the center of town. Mack's already hauling your luggage there."

"Er…that's good."

"You didn't think…I mean…did you want to stay here?" He raised an eyebrow in surprise.

"Oh, no. No. Of course not." Kay groaned inwardly. This was going horribly. They were both so afraid of making a mistake, they were treading on eggshells.

He returned to the living area, balancing two mugs of hot chocolate and a plate of cookies on a tray.

"I really am glad you changed your mind about coming to Alaska." He handed her a mug.

She took a sip of hot chocolate and nibbled on a cookie. The room was silent except for logs crackling in the fireplace.

"Cookies are good," she said as a way to fill the void.

"You can thank the Pillsbury Doughboy. All I did was slice and heat."

"Still, you sliced them very evenly and heated them to the perfect degree of doneness."

"Are you making fun of me?" His eyes teased.

Feeling suddenly shy, she glanced away. Oh, she was getting in way over her head here. Liking this guy too much, when they had no future together.

But she was in no position to ask for anything more from him than sex, nor did she want to. For one thing he was an Alaskan and she was a New Yorker. For another, she was on the rebound, still aching from Lloyd's betrayal. She had a lot of things to sort out before she could ever entertain a relationship that extended beyond the physical. With anyone.

Maybe coming here hadn't been such a great idea, after all.

Disconcerted, she moved away from Quinn and turned her attention to the photographs artfully arranged on the paneled wall on the opposite side of the room.

There was Quinn playing hockey. In another he was standing on the summit of Mount McKinley grinning like a happy kid. In a third he was kayaking. In a fourth he was guiding a group of tourists down white-water rapids in a rubber raft.

One picture caught her eye. It featured six muscular, bare-chested teenagers laughing and lobbing fistfuls of blueberries at each other. She recognized four of the boys from the magazine advertisement.

Quinn hadn't changed much. His hair was darker, his shoulders broader, but he still possessed the same insouciant grin and macho stance.

"That was the summer we all worked in Juneau taking tourists down the Mendenthall." He come up behind her and was standing so near she could almost feel his chin touching the top of her head. "We'd been picking blueberries and things got out of hand. My sister Meggie, the camera buff, sneaked up on us and snapped this photo."

"Who's that?" She pointed to a swarthy, dark-haired boy with straight white teeth.

"That's Jesse, Meggie's husband. They weren't married then, of course. In fact, I believe that was the summer Jesse's father married Caleb's mother."

"And this guy?" She pointed to a lanky, string-bean fellow whom Quinn had in a headlock while he smashed berries into his hair.

"That's Kyle."

"You two look like the best of friends."

"We were."

Something in his voice made Kay turn and look at him. "You're not friends anymore?"

Quinn shrugged. "I don't talk to him much. He met some girl who'd come to Alaska for the summer. Kyle fell head over heels. Moved to California for her. Haven't seen him in twelve years."

"You act like he betrayed you by falling in love."

Quinn cracked an uneasy smile. "It wasn't the falling-in-love part, it was the leaving Alaska. That woman put a ring in his nose, and he let her pull him around by it. Guess that's why I'm so determined to find a wilderness wife."

"Because you're not willing to compromise?"

"Not when it comes to leaving Alaska." He thrust his chest out as if he was proud of his stubbornness. "In fact, that's what happened to my last relationship. I asked Heather to marry me, but she refused to move to Bear Creek. I wasn't about to go to Cleveland where she lived. If a woman wants to love me, she's got to love Alaska, too. It's a package deal." He took a sip of his hot chocolate, then said, "You can quote me in your article."

Kay raised her eyebrows. With such an obstinate attitude the man might be hard-pressed to find his perfect mate. So why did she find his stubbornness attractive? Maybe it was the clear-cut, simple way he said what was on his mind and if people didn't like it, well, too bad. "I'll be sure to note that. Getting your story for the article is the reason I'm here."

"The only reason?" His eyes sought hers.

"No. It's not the only reason."

"No?" He gave her a quirky smile, which struck her the wrong way. As if he was feeling pretty cocky about his ability to attract her all the way across the continent.

"I needed to get out of the city after breaking things off with Lloyd."

"Ah." He grinned all the wider. "So you're no longer practically engaged."

"No, I'm not."

He smirked.

"Stop that."

"Stop what?"

"Looking so smug. My breaking up with Lloyd had nothing to do with you."

"I never said it did."

"Your expression implied it."

Why was she being so sensitive? What was the matter with her? For the past week, while she packed and made travel arrangements, she had been unable to think of anything but seeing Quinn again, and now that she was here, she was experiencing all kinds of conflicting emotions.

"I'm sorry," she said. "That sounded argumentative."

"Hey, I can handle it. If you need to get something off your chest, go right ahead."

Well, that was refreshing. He was ready to let her spew out her emotions. Her mother and her father and Lloyd encouraged her not to express her feelings. To keep things bottled up. Good little girls didn't let their anger show. She was damned tired of being good, and here was Quinn egging her on.

"You sure you're up for this?" She looked into his eyes, saw nothing but sincere interest and acceptance. She leaned forward and set her half-empty mug back on the tray.

"FYI for the article. I don't want a submissive yes-woman for a wife. I want a true partner who speaks her mind, shares her thoughts with me even though I might not agree with her. I'm a firm believer that passionate couples fight. As long as they fight fair. Hell, if you don't fight sometimes, if you agree about everything, where's the spark? Where's the passion?"

Kay gulped. Oh, yes. She had always felt the same

way. Just once when her father came home late, she had longed for her mother to confront him, throw a tantrum, demand he stop sleeping with other women. But Honoria had never once expressed her anger or voiced her opinion. Well-bred wives did not behave that way. Civilized-society women simply went shopping, spending extravagantly, consoling themselves with expensive but totally meaningless gewgaws.

And when she had tried to tell Lloyd her feelings or express her displeasure over something, he'd always headed her off, shut her down, closed her out, reminding her she was a Freemont with a certain level of dignity to maintain.

"You got something to tell me, Kay? Blast away, I'm listening."

Quinn gave her his full attention, his eyes on her face, his palms splayed over his thighs. Kay couldn't help but feel that the future Mrs. Scofield was going to be a very lucky woman—just as long as she was willing to move to Alaska.

"All right. It hurt my feelings when you turned down my offer at the Empire State Building. I don't go around inviting men into my bed willy-nilly. I just thought you should know that."

"I never thought you did."

"You thought I was terrible, wanting to cheat on my boyfriend."

"I didn't."

"You did."

He shook a finger. "Now don't go telling me what I thought."

"So what *did* you think about me?"

"I figured there must have been trouble in 'practically engaged' paradise for there to be so much attraction between us.''

''And?''

''I thought you were a beautiful, sexy woman who was obviously unhappy with her life and not getting what she needed from her primary relationships.''

Boy, he'd hit the nail on the head. Was she that obvious, or was he that observant?

''I think you're frustrated and disappointed and searching for something special.''

She ducked her head. This didn't feel very comfortable, having him analyze her and be so accurate.

He reached out and cupped her chin with his palm, raised her face to meet his gaze once more. ''I'd like to make you feel special, Kay.'' His expression was doing her in, causing her to feel hot and cold at the same time.

''Quinn, you're looking for a wife, and the last thing I'm in the market for is a husband.''

''Kay, I'm a pretty simple guy. I take life as I find it. I don't put expectations on people.''

''Then why did you reject me back in New York?''

''Like I told you then, I don't come between couples. You had to get free from Lloyd first before you could come to me. But you're here now. Officially unattached. Anything can happen.''

Anything.

The word reverberated in her head. It was exactly what she wanted to hear. Exactly what she feared most. By coming to Alaska she had set herself on a course of sexual exploration. If a man as virile as Quinn couldn't give her an orgasm, if he couldn't save her from a life of frustrated sexual fantasies, then could anyone?

QUINN DROVE KAY over to Jake's bed-and-breakfast in his parents' Wagoneer and gave her the keys. He'd started to walk her to the door, not wanting her to slip in the gloom and the snow, but she surprised him by announcing she wanted to walk around and check out the town.

"For the article," she explained.

They walked to the end of the half-mile-long boardwalk, which ended at the pier where the cruise ships docked in the summer. Most of the shops were closed for the winter, except for Long Bear's sundries and MacKenzie's trading post. He took her over to KCRK, his parents' radio station, and they waved to Liam Kilstrom who was in the control booth. They wandered past the community rec center and the nearby church, where the ladies' auxiliary was having a quilting bee. They strolled by the Happy Puffin bar, where half the town was hanging out, because it was trivia night. The other half of the town was either probably in Jake's huge sitting room or at the adjacent restaurant, Paradise Diner.

He was not quite certain what had passed between them at his house. Had she come to Alaska to have an affair with him or not? She wanted him as badly as he wanted her. He saw the desire reflected in her eyes, noticed her passion in the way she held her body, recognized longing in how she got flustered in his presence. But something was holding her back.

It was all he could do to keep from touching her, brushing a wisp of hair from her cheek, taking her hand to guide her over the icy patches on the road. He wanted to caress her and hold her and never let her go.

He had it bad and he knew that wasn't good. He

had to be careful. Kay was not a long-term relationship. He knew that. He didn't want either of them to get hurt. But man, how he wanted to make love to her.

His gut somersaulted and he drew in a deep, steadying breath, unable to remember when one woman had tied him so inextricably into knots. He was afraid of screwing up, of making a wrong move, of letting this one slip through his fingers. He wanted her with a power that shook his normal confidence.

Kay stopped on the wooden promenade, inhaled deeply of the cold air and gazed at the mountains surrounding the town.

"It's so incredibly beautiful here," she murmured. "Breathtaking. Overwhelming. Majestic. Totally wild. Honestly, I had no idea."

"It's just home to me." He grinned.

"I can't believe how different it is from New York. Bear Creek is quaint and clean and charming. No noise, no pollution, no panhandlers. I've got to tell you the truth, all this quiet is a shock to my system. How do you stand it?"

"How do you stand Manhattan?"

She gave a little laugh, and the delicate, feminine sound drilled a corkscrew of awareness straight through his groin. "I suppose it's what you're accustomed to. Although I've got to admit it can be a tough place to live. I've been mugged twice in two years."

"That's awful."

She shrugged. "Builds character."

"I hate the thought of someone accosting you," he said vehemently. "Makes me want to do bodily harm."

"Omigosh!" she exclaimed, and latched on to his arm.

"What is it?"

"There's a moose. Trotting right down Main Street. I was reading a book on Alaska on the flight over, and it said moose are often more dangerous than bears. Is that true?"

"Moose have been known to cause a lot of damage."

"Do they bite?"

Quinn struggled not to laugh. Her gloved fingers dug into his forearm. Her lithe body trembled against his. Ah, at last, here was his opportunity to touch her, even if he had to do something a little underhanded to keep her latched on to him.

"Shh. Hang on to me, Kay. We'll tiptoe past him and hopefully he won't notice us."

"Quinn—" her voice warbled and her eyes grew round as hubcaps "—maybe we should turn around and go back to the pier. Give him the whole street."

The moose snorted and trotted closer.

"Oh! Oh!"

"I'll protect you." He thrust her behind him.

Her arms went around his waist and her sweet-smelling head popped out from under the crook of his arm so she could keep her eyes fixed on the moose.

"He's huge," she whispered. "What if he charges?"

"I'll hold him off while you run away."

"Quinn, I'm scared."

He patted her hand. "It's all right, Kay. I won't let any harm come to you. This isn't New York."

The moose snorted and pawed the ground. Then raised his shaggy head and glared at them.

Kay tightened her grip on his waist.

"We'll just ease on by." Quinn took a tentative step forward.

''No, no.'' She dug in her heels. ''Please don't move.''

The moose chose that moment to turn and lope off in the opposite direction. Kay sighed and sagged against his body. ''Whew. That was a close call.''

Reprobate, his conscience accused. *Tell her the truth.*

''Kay...'' he began, but she was no longer next to him. She was sprinting toward Jake's B&B. He had to run to catch up with her.

She wrenched open the door and tumbled headlong into the foyer.

The place was packed with toddy-sipping locals gathered around a roaring fire, playing chess, swapping tall tales, listening to the weather report on the radio. The minute Kay burst through the entryway, every head turned to stare at her, and he hated the way they gawked.

''Wild moose!'' Kay gasped. ''Walking down Main Street.''

The denizens of Bear Creek, mostly men, all Quinn's neighbors and friends, stared at her as if she was some exotic bird who'd migrated too far north. More than a few mouths dropped open, and even Lulu, Jake's Siberian husky, lifted her head off the rug. A twinge of guilt bit him for having let her believe the moose was dangerous.

''Well,'' Kay demanded, sinking her hands on her hips and glaring about her, ''aren't you guys going to do something about it?''

The room broke into raucous laughter.

Kay blushed and pivoted on her heel to face Quinn. ''What's so funny?''

"Quinn got you thinkin' that moose is a killer?" cackled an old fellow seated at a table near the door, a chessboard on the table in front of him.

"Don't let old Gus give you a hard time," soothed a handsome man that Kay recognized from the publicity photo Quinn had shown her in New York. He had sandy hair and a boyish grin that promised lots of fun. "That's just Kong, our resident moose. Caleb bottle-fed him from the time he was a calf. His Momma got hit by an RV during tourist season five years ago. Kong's tamer than a poodle."

"Oh." She felt like fifty different kinds of fool. Why had Quinn let her believe the moose was dangerous? She glared at him, and he had the good sense to look ashamed of himself.

"I get it, ha, ha, ha. Play a trick on the city girl."

"I'm sorry." Quinn jammed his hands in his pockets.

"It's okay. I can take a joke."

"I'm Jake, by the way. You must be Kay." Quinn's buddy held out his hand. "We've heard a lot about you. Welcome to Bear Creek."

"Thank you, Jake." She shook his hand and smiled graciously, determined to regain her dignity.

"Would you like me to show you to your room?" Jake asked.

"That would be lovely."

"This way."

Jake led her up the wide cedar staircase to a room decorated with rustic charm. Quinn started to trail after them, but Kay turned and planted a palm on his chest. "Excuse me, big man, but I don't recall anyone inviting you up to my room."

6

"SHE SURE PUT YOU in your place," Jake teased Quinn when he returned to the B&B three hours after Kay had kicked him out. Lulu lay on the rug at his feet, eyeing Quinn with the same amusement that was evident in her owner's face.

"Oh, shut up."

"Quinn's got a girlfriend."

"Grow up," Quinn growled, and scowled.

He had gone home to give her time to cool off and to prepare a peace offering, and he'd come back to restlessly pace the corridor of the B&B, trying to gather his courage to knock on Kay's door. Since when could one feisty little woman make his knees quake?

He pushed his fingers through his hair and let out a long breath, which did nothing to ease the nervousness and self-reproach squeezing his gut. If he wasn't careful he was going to mess things up royally with Kay.

He had fibbed to her, inadvertently embarrassed her, and that had never been his intent. He had to apologize, get back into her good graces.

Resolutely he knocked on her door.

"Should I go get Meggie?" Jake asked. "Just in case Kay decides to slam-dunk you down the staircase and you need the services of a trained RN?"

"Beat it." Quinn glowered at his friend.

Chuckling to himself, Jake sauntered off, Lulu on his heels.

And Kay answered the door. ''Oh. Are you still here?''

''Can we talk?''

She crossed her arms over her chest. ''So talk.''

''In private.'' He waved a hand. ''Eavesdroppers are rampant around here.''

She shook her head and studied him for a long moment. Should she stay mad? He gave her a sad expression. She opened her door wider. ''All right.''

Quinn scooted over the threshold.

Kay shut the door behind him, then turned to face him. ''Did you have fun embarrassing me in front of all your friends?''

''It wasn't like that.''

''Wasn't like what? I was terrified of that moose!'' She punched him lightly on the shoulder. He arched his eyebrows in surprise. She wasn't given to admitting feelings of weakness, and the fact that she had done so amazed her. But darn it, she had been scared.

''You told me you'd survived two muggings and it was no big deal. Why would a moose scare you?'' Quinn looked genuinely puzzled.

''Because it's the unknown. Why did you let me make a fool of myself?''

''I had no idea you were going to rush into Jake's and call everyone to arms against Kong. What can I say? I liked it when you grabbed on to me, when you needed me to protect you.''

''Really?'' She slanted him a sideways glance. She was flattered and she probably shouldn't be, but truthfully it had made her feel very feminine to know this brawny man could protect her from wild creatures.

"Yeah. I am sorry—I acted like a jerk, Kay."

Her name on his tongue tracked an unstoppable awareness through her. She pressed a hand to her stomach to still the fluttering there. A man who could admit when he was wrong? Unbelievable.

"Forgive me?"

"You're forgiven," she said.

"Forgiven enough so that you'll agree to have dinner with me?"

"All right." She nodded. "Just let me change."

"I'll wait for you in the lobby."

Grinning, Quinn hurried back downstairs. Thank heavens she'd accepted his dinner invitation. He'd gone all out, preparing his famous salmon chowder, putting Coltrane on the CD player, chilling a bottle of champagne. He hoped he wasn't going overboard or pushing too hard.

His stomach took a dive at the thought. He'd never felt so out of his element with a woman. He was used to cocking a seductive grin at the ladies and having them tumble right into his bed. Why this one caused him to doubt himself, he had no idea.

Maybe because he wanted her so badly.

A few minutes later Kay floated down the staircase. Once again every eye in the room was trained on her lithe, graceful form. Even Lulu thumped her tail approvingly from her place by the fire.

Quinn gulped. He could only stare, bug-eyed. She wore a black velvet long-sleeved dress and black high-heeled fashion boots. Not exactly Alaskan wear, but damn, those boots did fine things for her legs.

In that moment he flashed back to the first time he'd seen her on the plane. He recalled the way her legs looked encased in silk stockings. A rampant forest fire suddenly blazed through him, and he was at a loss for words.

The bodice of her dress clung snugly to her full breasts. The skirt swished seductively when she moved.

As she descended the last step, he stood up to greet her.

"Are you going to be warm enough in that outfit?" he asked.

She leaned in close, the hair on the top of her head tickling his nose. "Shh, don't tell anyone. I have on long-handled underwear."

That secret should have killed his libido-fed fantasies about satin and lace covering her silky skin. Instead he found himself even more aroused by the thought of her in cotton flannel. Perspiration beaded his brow.

He was a sick, sick man.

The sky was inky black as they walked to the SUV. This time of year they got only about five hours of daylight. He carried a flashlight and shone it over the parking lot to light their way, while keeping his arm firmly locked around Kay's waist. He wasn't about to let anything happen to her.

"I can't believe how dark it is," she whispered. "No streetlights. No cars on the road. Quiet as a cemetery."

He tried to see Bear Creek from her point of view and failed. He considered the darkness comforting, the vastness of the landscape inspiring.

"Where are we going?" she asked.

"My place."

"Not to a restaurant?" Her voice rose on the question, as if she was nervous about his reply.

"The only restaurant open during the winter months is the Paradise Diner next to the B&B. You'll be sick enough of it by the time you head back to New York."

"Only one restaurant? You've got to be kidding."

"I'm not. Bear Creek's winter population is about fifteen hundred."

"And in the summer?"

"Late May through mid-August the population swells to three, four thousand, double that when the cruise ships are in town."

"Wow."

They arrived at his cabin, and he escorted her inside and took her coat.

"Something smells wonderful!" she exclaimed. "I'm starving."

"Salmon chowder and grilled sourdough bread."

"Sounds delicious."

"Made it myself. The chowder that is, not the bread."

She laughed.

Once in the kitchen, she enthused over the tablecloth, the candles, the champagne just as he'd hoped, and Quinn began to relax. He'd pleased her, which was precisely his intent.

He pulled back her chair for her. She smiled up at him. They ate and talked and ate and talked as if they'd been friends for a thousand years.

Quinn couldn't quit staring at her. Whenever her pink tongue flicked out to take a morsel of food from her spoon, it felt as if she was licking him in a very private place. Several times he had to bite down on his bottom lip to keep from groaning out loud.

Kay was impressed that he'd worked so hard to make such a delicious meal. She admired his impeccable table manners and sent sideways glances at him. The candlelight accented his features. He'd rolled up his sleeves while serving their dinner, exposing those magnificent forearms that drove her wild with desire.

"So, Quinn, for the sake of the readers of *Metropolitan* magazine, what's your idea of the perfect date?" she asked, desperate to get her mind off his extreme sexiness.

"We're back to the article again."

"Yes."

"We're having it."

"What?"

"The perfect date." He reached across the table, laid a hand on hers. "Good food. Great conversation. A pretty woman."

"Oh." Taken aback by the very bold look in his eyes, Kay removed her hand from underneath his.

"There's only one thing that would make it better."

She held her breath.

"Dessert."

He disappeared into the kitchen for a few minutes and then brought out baked Alaska.

"You made this yourself?" she gasped as he set the flaming dessert in front of her.

"It's not as hard as it looks."

"I'm impressed."

"That was my intent."

He nailed her with his steady gaze.

She'd never met a man like Quinn. At once extremely masculine, yet oddly enough quite domestic. He possessed a self-confidence that would attract any woman. He had an intense strength underlying his every action, and hey, the guy could even admit when he was wrong. She wagered that mere weeks after his advertisement ran in the magazine, he'd be well on his way to matrimony with the wild woman of his dreams.

She experienced a strange tug in her belly. Was she actually jealous of that as-yet-nonexistent woman?

You don't have to be jealous. You can have him for now. He's the tonic to soothe your shattered ego. So what if there's no happily-ever-after? What about happily-right-now?

They ate the baked Alaska; then Quinn wiped his mouth with his napkin, checked his watch and shoved back his chair. "It's about time."

"Time for what?"

"Come with me. There's something I'd like to show you." He got to his feet and held out his hand to her. "This way."

He guided her toward the stairs.

Toward the bedroom?

Kay gulped. Was she really ready for this? She had taken the assignment because she wanted to see Quinn again. And because she couldn't stop lusting after him, but when push came to shove, could she go through with it?

"Quinn...I..."

He placed a finger to her lips. "Shh."

His finger tasted slightly salty, the pressure of it against her mouth startlingly arousing. She had the strongest urge to capture that finger with her teeth and suck.

He cocked his head and smiled oh-so-slightly, as if miraculously reading her thoughts. The five-o'clock shading riding his jaw looked rough, exciting, and she wondered what it would feel like rasping against her cheek.

In a split second she was locked in another fantasy.

She envisioned him without his clothes on and hiccuped at the image that rose to her mind. He would look gorgeous naked. She just knew it. Golden skin, perfectly defined muscles, firm hiney.

Kay gulped.

"Come," he urged. "Come."

Did she dare?

Maybe, Kay realized, maybe she was afraid of finding out that she really was sexually dysfunctional. But how could she be frigid when she felt so hot and wet and achy deep inside? When her entire body begged for a release she'd dreamed about on a daily basis?

He laced his fingers through hers and, walking backward, slowly pulled her up the first step. "I'm not going to bite," he murmured. "Unless you want me to."

Her heart punched her rib cage as she placed one booted foot on the first hardwood step.

His gaze snagged hers and held on tight. Kay shivered at the purely masculine gleam in his sultry eyes. Even from arm's length, she could feel his body heat radiating outward.

She was coming undone. Something uncoiled in her belly. Something soft and warm and messy.

His breathing, husky with desire, echoed loudly in the confines of the staircase. The erotic sound strummed along her nerve endings, escalating her excitement. She struggled to draw in a steady breath of her own, but ended up panting shallowly, her eyes locked to his.

Up another step and then another.

Scalding hot. It must be 110 degrees in here. Quinn tightened his grip on her fingers. She needed to run outside and roll around in the snow.

"Almost there," he coaxed.

Almost where? His bedroom? At the thought she experienced this incredible, inextricable push-pull. Her nipples tightened in anticipation; she could feel them protruding against the material of her bra. Pressure, sweet, sweet pressure, grew between her legs.

"Here we are," he said at last, and she mounted the last step.

But where he led her was not a bedroom.

Kay blinked.

It was another spacious living area with rafter ceilings, a second fireplace, leather couch, braided rug. A handmade quilt graced the back of the couch. The far corner housed a desk complete with computer, printer, fax, copier and scanner.

Outdoor and rescue equipment hung from pegs mounted along the paneling or were in organized rows on built-in shelves. Harnesses, ropes, pulleys and crampons for mountain climbing. Life vests, oars and wading boots for river rafting. There were fire extinguishers and first-aid kits, a citizens band radio and a huge stash of flashlights. Obviously this was his office.

But what grabbed her attention and held her transfixed was the plate-glass window running along one wall overlooking the bay and the incredible display on view.

Kay's hand rose to her throat as she stared at the brilliant curtain of shimmering green, red and white that fluttered ghostlike across the sky. She had never seen anything so awe-inspiring as those radiant spectral waves.

The shimmers danced and twirled, gauzy curtains of brilliant brightness changing shapes, billowing out like a green genie from a bottle in those old cartoons she had been banned from watching as a child.

"The northern lights," she whispered.

"Yeah." His voice was as husky with awe and respect as her own.

"It's incredible. Resplendent. Superlative. Words can't began to describe it."

"Nature's light show. We see the aurora up to two hundred times a year from early spring to late fall. This year promises to be particularly vibrant because of increased sunspot activity."

"What causes this spectacle?"

"Scientifically speaking," Quinn said, "the northern lights are electrical discharges resulting from the interaction between wind and the earth's magnetic field."

"Oh."

"But the Native Alaskans believe the lights were torches carried by old souls to guide the new souls into the next world."

A carpet of gooseflesh covered her arms, despite her long-handled underwear. She felt shivery inside and not just from the eerie legend, but from her closeness to Quinn.

He'd brought her up here to see this breathtaking display, not to make love to her. She was simultaneously relieved and disappointed.

Kiss me, she thought. *Kiss me now, kiss me hard, kiss me long.*

But she didn't say those things. Instead, she turned to him and smiled softly, belying the inner turmoil raging through her mind. "Thank you, Quinn, for showing this to me."

"You're welcome. Hang on, I'll get us some champagne and we'll toast your arrival and the appearance of the sometimes temperamental aurora. I'd hoped she would come out to play tonight, but you never know for certain."

"She?"

"The aurora is most definitely a feminine force," he said. "Watch the sky. See how the lights flicker and tease? She's fickle. Coming on hot, then shying away. Coyly fading one minute, flaring boldly the next. Cool yet strangely hot. Oh, Aurora is a woman all right. She's got many moods."

"You're quite the romantic," Kay said.

"So I've been told."

"I still don't understand why you're not married." She shook her head.

"Hopefully your article and our ad will help rectify that."

But I don't want you to get married, a selfish little voice inside her cried. *If you get married, you can't be my boy-toy.*

She watched him amble to the champagne bucket positioned next to the stereo system. He turned on the radio, and the sound of Wilson Picket's "Midnight Hour" spun out into the room.

"Oh," she said, "I love this song."

"That's KCRK," Quinn told her. "I put together the play list for tonight."

He wrangled with the champagne bottle. She heard the cork pop, watched him fill two flutes with fizzy champagne.

"You went to a lot of trouble for me."

His eyes met hers as he handed her a flute. "You're worth it."

Blinking up at his handsome face, Kay noticed

things she hadn't paid attention to before—the way his brown hair, shot through with golden strands, curled slightly over his forehead, the way his eyes went soft and seemed to caress her, the tiny mole an inch above the left side of his mouth.

He raised his glass. "To the moment," he murmured.

She clinked the lip of hers against the lip of his. "To the moment."

They sipped their champagne, eyed each other over the rim of their glasses. Kay felt at once heavy and yet extremely light, like a helium balloon tied to a child's wrist. Weighted but yearning to fly.

Suddenly she burped.

"Oh, my goodness!" she exclaimed, and slapped a hand over her mouth. In her family burping aloud was a sin akin to indecent exposure. "I'm so embarrassed. Please forgive me."

"Lighten up, sweetheart. What's to forgive? So you burped. Actually it makes me feel better. I was beginning to think you were too perfect."

"I'm not perfect. Not by a long shot."

"Well, if burping on champagne is your biggest fault, I won't kick you out of my bed."

Their eyes met, held for a long moment.

"Come sit." He eased down on the couch, patted the cushion next to him.

She sat down beside him. He stretched his arm out over the back of the couch. She was acutely aware of it resting there. She imagined his fingers tangling in her hair, his mouth devouring hers. Briefly she closed her eyes and when she opened them again, she focused on the dancing lights beyond the window.

Quinn studied Kay as she watched the northern

lights. Her profile mesmerized him. Her nose was refined, her cheekbones sculpted. Just looking at her made his heart feel crooked, as if it had slipped in his chest.

Her scent teased his nostrils. Warm and rich and compelling, it smelled of something foreign and exotic. Was that what attracted him to her? She was like no other woman of his acquaintance.

Her hair brushed lightly across his skin. He noticed her perfectly manicured fingernails, the delicate shape of her hands, her narrow wrist decorated with a gold tennis bracelet. Even though she was right beside him, she still seemed detached somehow. Her detachment intrigued him just as it had on the airplane.

Her aloofness roused him, made him want to do something drastic to bring her into the fold. She had lived in New York too long, spent too much time disconnected from people, too often kept her feelings to herself. Her two-week stay in Bear Creek would do her a world of good. Help her open up to herself and the world around her. He wondered if he should tell her about his urge to rattle her cage, ruffle her feathers, crack her facade. He ached to tell her exactly how he hoped to liberate her. But Quinn feared that if he spoke these words, it would be a mistake from which he could never recover.

And yet he felt driven, nervous. His heart began a fretful pounding. There were no words for what he wanted to say, and his tongue lay paralyzed on the floor of his mouth. A knot of pressure built inside him. Pressure that urged him to haul her into his arms and show her everything he simply could not say.

He wasn't good with flowery sentiment. He was a

man of action, and only action could quiet his restlessness. His body tensed and he leaned in close.

She looked at him then, her pale hair gleaming in the firelight, rivaling the natural phenomena flickering outside the window. Her breathing was shallow, and her brown eyes shone with a fevered effervescence. He'd never seen anything so lovely.

Kay felt his body shift toward her, pressing her deeper into the plush leather couch. His left side was crushed against her right, and he placed a hand on her thigh. Then his mouth was on hers—oh, how she had dreamed of kissing him again—urgent and insistent. She was concurrently both hot and cold. His body was tense, hard, but his lips were soft, inviting.

And his tongue.

Dear Lord, it ought to be illegal to possess such a tongue!

From there everything went wild, flailed totally out of control. He dropped his arm from the back of the couch, wrapped it around her waist and hauled her against his body, forcing her to spread her knees.

She felt his erection through his pants. It throbbed against her belly with a provocative rhythm. They were fused. Lips to lips. Chest to chest. Thigh to thigh. And yet it wasn't nearly close enough. Too much clothing in the way.

Twining her fingers into the warm, thick, whiskey-colored hair at the nape of his neck, she arched her body against his. She opened her mouth wider, encouraging that roving tongue to pepper her with wet, sexual thrusts.

He mimicked her moves, one hand cupping the back of her neck. The fingers of his other hand stroked her jaw, her throat and skimmed lower until he was caressing her breasts through the velvety bodice of her dress. He kneaded the pliant flesh, searing her with triple-digit heat. Oh, she couldn't wait until his hands were on her bare skin.

His thumb flicked across the pebble-hard nipple straining tight against her restrictive clothing. Damn, but she wanted to be naked. She threw back her head and a needy moan escaped her lips.

Putty. She was nothing but putty in his hands. The notion both frightened and exhilarated her.

Feverish desire clawed through her, pulling her down, drawing her under the power of Quinn's spell. With the aurora borealis whipping gracefully in her peripheral vision, the fireplace embers glowing and Quinn's tongue on its restless pursuit, she felt swept away by some unstoppable, forbidden fantasy.

Except this reality was more titillating than her most taboo dreams.

Too much torture. She simply could not stand this any longer. She wanted him. Now. Crazily, illogically, this very minute. She refused to stub out her urges. Passion pushed all her fears aside. Desire evaporated any shred of common sense she might have possessed. She wrenched her mouth from his.

"Quinn," she gasped. "Before we go any further, there's something I must tell you."

He looked dazed, muzzy with craving. Their breathing mingled in rapid spurts.

"What is it?"

"I'm not..." She paused, not quite certain how to put this. "I'm not like other women."

"You got that right, sweetheart." He couldn't seem to resist dropping a kiss on her jaw. That achingly light pressure threw her completely off-kilter.

She splayed a hand on his chest and pushed him back. She needed a moment to regroup. "No. I don't mean it like that."

He rearranged himself on the couch, shoved a hand through his hair and gave her his complete attention. "I'm listening."

"I've never..." She squirmed uncomfortably. She hated admitting her deficiencies. She'd been raised on the myth that Freemonts never revealed their flaws. So why was she going to tell him her darkest secret? Because she felt as if he was the only one who could help her. "Well...you know..."

"What? Had sex?" He stared at her in disbelief.

"I'm twenty-seven, Quinn. I was almost engaged. Of course I've had sex."

"Oh. What then?" He frowned.

This was so hard. She squirmed, she fidgeted. She tried the words out mentally first, but nothing seemed right. Finally she blurted, "I've never..." Then paused again.

"Never what?"

She dropped her voice to a whisper. "...had an orgasm."

"You're kidding. For real?"

She nodded. "Lloyd says I'm frigid. That it's my fault he had to turn to other women."

"Bullshit!" Quinn spoke with such vehemence, Kay jumped. "Sorry, I didn't mean to scare you. But that ex-boyfriend of yours is a jerk."

His anger at Lloyd flattered her. She knew then that she had done the right thing by coming to Alaska, by revealing to Quinn her hidden shame.

"How he could fool around on such a beautiful,

exciting, interesting woman is beyond me. He must have sawdust for brains."

"You think I'm interesting?" She smiled shyly, not meaning to be coy. She wasn't milking him for more compliments, but she was touched beyond measure that he found her interesting, as she'd always thought herself rather dull.

"Interesting, hell." Quinn snorted. "You're downright mysterious. You keep yourself so contained. I ache to know what you're thinking when you get those Mona Lisa smiles on your face. And you're anything but frigid. If you've never been able to come, it's through no fault of your own. You've just been with the wrong men."

Kay gulped. This next part was hard, but she had to say it. "I want to ask a favor of you."

"What is it?" His eyes never left her face.

"Do you think that maybe you could help me…er… achieve sexual fulfillment?"

"Say the word, sweetheart," he encouraged her, lifting a hand to capture a strand of her hair and rub it between his fingers. "Put aside that aristocratic breeding of yours and tell me that you want to come bigger than the state of Alaska."

Pressing her teeth into her bottom lip, she stared straight into his eyes.

And almost lost it completely.

"I want you to make me come," she begged him. "More than anything in the world."

7

HOW HAD HE GOTTEN so lucky?

Kay Freemont, rich, successful, cultured and beautiful, wanted to entrust him, a simple Alaskan man, with her sexual awakening.

Stunned, delighted, touched, flattered and horny beyond comprehension. How had he gotten so lucky?

He sent a brief prayer of thanks to the heavens and added a pleading postscript: *Don't let me lose control. Help me to be strong so I can give her what she needs.*

It was going to be hard—pun definitely intended—to rein in his own ravenous desires. He hadn't been with a woman since he and Heather had broken up. He was hanging by a thread.

But he had to dig deep, find a way to put his own needs on hold. Because Kay was giving him the opportunity of a lifetime. She was granting him the privilege of bringing her to the heights of her sexuality.

He was a fortunate SOB and he would not let her down.

She took a long swallow of champagne, then sat her glass on the floor at her feet and shifted her body into his. "I'm ready, Quinn. Make love to me."

Shaking his head, he reached out and tenderly traced her lips with his thumb. She shivered beneath his caress, and the shot of adrenaline that jumped into his gut floored him.

Control, Scofield. Control.

"Oh, no, my sweet, not so fast," Quinn said, when what he wanted to do more than anything in the world was strip that velvet dress over her head, rip off those long johns and make messy, wet, hot love to her.

"What do you mean?" she whispered, her eyes growing wide.

"A proper seduction takes time."

"Oh, yes? How much time?" She seemed alarmed.

"Depends."

"On what?"

He grinned wickedly. "When you're ready."

"I'm ready tonight," she said a bit peevishly. She narrowed her eyes at him and he understood her frustration. If she thought she was frustrated now, she was in for a big shock.

"No, you're not."

"Yes, I am."

"Listen, sweetheart, we're doing this my way or not at all. Got that?"

She glared at him, crossed her arms over her chest, flipped one knee over the other. "I'm not sure I like this."

"Before I make love to you, you'll have to eject that uptight demeanor."

"I'm not uptight."

"Arms crossed, legs crossed. Babe, you're closed up tighter than Glacier Bay in January."

"So you *do* think I'm frigid."

"No! Okay, that was a bad analogy. I do not think you're frigid. But in order for you to get the full sexual experience, you're going to have to relax. And before you can do that, you're going to have to trust me completely."

"And how long will this take?" she asked, purposely uncrossing both her arms and her legs to show she was ready, willing and able to start trusting and relaxing right now.

He lowered his head, his mouth almost on hers. He smelled the fruity scent of champagne on her lips. Right then and there he almost caved. He barely resisted the urge to capture that sassy mouth with his once more.

"Don't worry," he whispered huskily. "You'll know."

EXHAUSTION CLAIMED her mind, haunted her body. Kay had spent the rest of the night in her lonely bed at Jake Gerard's B&B pining for a man who was bent on serving up sweet torture.

And in between the tossing and turning, she had been consumed with rampant fantasies about Quinn. In one scenario he was a wild-eyed pirate who kidnapped and savaged her repeatedly in the hold of his ship. In another fantasy she was a domineering amazon who kept him chained in the basement for her pleasure. In yet another vision he was a wounded soldier fighting for the other side, and she was a caring nursemaid who hid him in her father's barn.

Ack!

She was slowly losing her ever-loving mind. She had to stop thinking about Quinn. She had work to do. An article to write. She was going to get dressed, go out on the town and explore Bear Creek. She refused to dwell on the fact that he wouldn't make love to her yet and put her out of her misery.

Groaning, she threw back the covers and crept out of bed, stripping off her nightgown and heading straight for the shower. Standing under the stream of hot water, she kept thinking about what Quinn had said.

You're not ready.

Well, how the hell did he know what she was ready for? He barely knew her. But in a way that was what made this whole venture so exciting. Knowing she would never see him again after her trip to Alaska, having this fabulous memory of her sexual adventure and possessing a wistful fondness for the man who showed her that she was all woman. This knowledge was the only thing that had given her the courage to express her true desires to him. To ask him to become her mentor in love.

So here she was, with her fanny on the line, ready, willing and able for action. And Quinn had been the one to put the brakes on.

She soaped her hair but in an instant she was fantasizing again. She saw Quinn in the shower, massaging the shampoo into her scalp, then rinsing her hair.

Her belly clenched with heated desire as she envisioned his hard body brushing hers, his manhood standing at attention. He would press her against the cool tile while hot water sluiced over their fevered skin. He would claim her mouth with his. Roughly, insistently, pillaging her territory. Then he would change tempo and the kisses would turn long and soft and lazy.

She arches her body into his. Desperate for release. She begs him to enter her. She needs to feel him inside her. Needs to experience the fullness only his large shaft will bring.

His fingers curl into the most private part of her. He rubs her cleft gently at first, then with more pressure.

Her sensitive breasts tighten and swell in response, and he gloats over her hardened nipples, taking credit for her arousal. He dips his head to those perky mounds, taking first one into his mouth and then turning his attention to the other. He flicks his tongue over the pink peak. It's as if there is a string connecting her nipples to her groin. With each seductive lick she feels a deepening ache at her very center.

She bites her bottom lip to keep from crying out, but he urges her to let go.

"Scream if you want," he insists, his mouth against her ear. "Let the world know we're making love."

Then he's nibbling her earlobe, running his silky tongue along the outside of her ear. The shudder that crawls through her rocks her to her core. She wraps her arms around his neck, clings to him....

The hot water gone cold forced her back to reality.

Kay opened her eyes, found her lips were pressed against the wall tile. Chagrined, she hopped backward, slipped and would have crashed to the floor of the tub if she hadn't grasped the soap rack.

Oh, she was pathetic. If Quinn didn't make love to her soon, she would explode into a million pieces. That would go over big on the New York social register—and with her mother!

Shaking her head, Kay turned off the water, eased out of the shower and wrapped a towel around herself.

Okay. No more nonsense. She was going to stop thinking about Quinn. She had work to do.

Twenty minutes later she was in the Paradise Diner enjoying blueberry pancakes and surrounded by a curious contingency of Bear Creek's entertaining citizens.

Kay knew she was a novelty, and they were asking

her more questions than she was asking them. Jake Gerard introduced her to Caleb Greenleaf, the only wife-hunting bachelor she hadn't yet met.

Caleb turned out to be a serious man with almost unbelievable good looks. It took a lot of coaxing, but after a while he told her about his job as a naturalist for the state of Alaska. He was quite different from his buddies. Introverted, where the other three were clearly extroverts.

Everyone in Bear Creek was friendly, open, welcoming, so very unlike some of the New Yorkers she knew, who had a tendency to be curt, suspicious and unimpressed. They enthusiastically told her many things about their lives. They were so trusting. Too trusting, to her way of thinking. But that's what she liked most about them.

Her New York life seemed very far away, and she couldn't think of anything she missed.

Later, after she'd already compiled copious notes and recorded more than three hours worth of conversations, an attractive, middle-aged couple, holding hands and grinning at each other as if they shared the secret to long-term romance, came in for lunch.

The woman stepped carefully, slowed by a booted walking cast on her right foot. Her husband solicitously helped her up to the counter. They sat on Kay's left, the man taking the stool Caleb had vacated.

He held out his hand to her and gave her a friendly smile. ''Jim Scofield. We just had to come over to meet the reporter our son coaxed to come here all the way from New York City.''

''You're Quinn's parents? Thanks so much for letting me use your extra car.'' Kay ran a hand self-consciously through her hair. She hadn't bothered to blow-dry and style it that morning since she knew she would be wearing a woolen cap much of the day, but now she wished she had. Skimping on her grooming was not normal for her, and she felt exposed and at a disadvantage, even though she had already discovered most of the women in Bear Creek didn't wear makeup or style their hair. Everything from their chunky Gore-Tex boots to their sensible parkas were geared for warmth and comfort. You'd never find a fashion show in Bear Creek.

"Yep." Jim slung his arm over the woman's shoulder. "This is my wife, Linda."

"You did a fine job raising your son," Kay told them as she shook their hands.

"We're pretty proud of him." When Linda smiled, her gray eyes softened into welcoming crinkles, just like Quinn's. "And our daughter, Meggie. She's an emergency-room nurse at a children's hospital in Seattle. She's visiting for a couple of weeks to help me while I'm out of commission." Linda gestured at her cast. "You and Meggie ought to get together. She's a city girl just like you, and I do believe you two are the only single women in town under thirty and over eighteen."

"I'd love to meet her."

Kay felt a tug of sadness in her heart, and she couldn't really say why. Maybe because this couple were so different from her own parents. They wore woolen pants, nylon and flannel, where Honoria and Charles Freemont were never seen in public without being impeccably dressed.

Linda and Jim sent each other private signals with their eyes. Kay's parents rarely even looked each other in the face. The Scofields touched frequently with simple, loving gestures. Her mother and father were rarely even in the same room together.

Without any encouragement, Quinn's parents extolled his virtues.

"Did you know Quinn's on the volunteer fire department?" Linda asked.

"No, I didn't." Kay scribbled on her notepad, *Bet he looks good in fire boots and suspenders and nothing else.*

"He's captain of the local hockey team," Jim bragged.

"Quinn has a bachelor's degree in sports physiology," Linda said.

"He's owned his own business for ten years and each year he turns a bigger profit." Jim nodded.

"And he still finds time to help us out at the radio station. You couldn't ask for a better son." Linda took a sip of her coffee. "Or better husband material. Write that down." She waved a hand at Kay's notebook. "I'm hoping this advertisement thing pays off for Quinn. I'm ready for grandchildren, and Meggie doesn't seem to be in any hurry to accommodate me."

Jim eyed Kay. "You wouldn't be interested in our boy yourself, would you? You're a beautiful young lady. You two would have the handsomest kids."

"Oh, no." Kay struggled to tamp down the telltale blush she knew was spreading up her neck. "I mean, I like Quinn very much, but I'm a New Yorker. And I just got out of a relationship. I'm not ready for anything serious. Quinn and I are at two different places in our lives."

Immediately she realized she'd given too much information too quickly. Why had she said so much? That certainly wasn't like her, spilling her guts to strangers. Probably she'd spouted off because she didn't want them getting the wrong idea about Quinn and her.

But oddly enough, her nervous revelation seemed to endear her to Quinn's parents. The Scofields smiled at her sweetly and Jim patted her on the shoulder. "No explanation necessary."

"But you do like him," Linda said.

Oh, great. How had she gotten herself into this conversation?

"Mom, Dad," Quinn boomed from the door of the restaurant, "stop bending Kay's ear."

Relieved, Kay looked up to see him stalk toward them. Her heart gave this strange little thump and she suddenly felt all loose and melty inside. He was even better-looking than she remembered in that hard-edged, masculine way of his.

He stopped beside her stool. "Hey."

"Hey, yourself." Inwardly she cringed. That sounded too flirty.

"Sleep well?" He grinned as if he knew she hadn't slept a wink.

"Considering the circumstances."

"Strange bed and all that."

"And all that," she echoed.

"We better be heading out." Jim Scofield got to his feet, left some money on the counter, then turned to help his wife from her stool. "Linda's got a doctor's appointment in Anchorage at two-thirty, and Mack's waiting to fly us over, so we better get a move on. Nice meeting you, Kay."

"Nice to meet you, too." She wriggled her fingers at them.

"Quinn, you must bring Kay to dinner on Saturday

night,'' Linda insisted. ''We're having a little get-together.''

''Thank you, Mrs. Scofield. I'd love to come.''

Linda whispered something in Quinn's ear and nudged him in the ribs.

''All right, Mom. We'll be there.''

''What'd she say?'' Kay asked after his parents had left the restaurant. Quinn perched on the stool beside her.

''She said I was supposed to be nice to you.''

''Oh, really?''

''She likes you.''

''How can you tell?''

''I just know.''

''I like her, too. I like both your folks.''

Kay couldn't help but think about her own parents again. Honoria and Charles would be as rejecting of Quinn as his parents were accepting of her. The vast differences between them yawned before her. Good thing her relationship with Quinn was purely sexual. They wouldn't have to deal with sticky things like disappointed in-laws. Best leave that to the bachelorettes who would come pouring into Bear Creek with marriage on their minds.

''I dropped by to see if you'd like to come over tomorrow night,'' Quinn said.

''Tomorrow? Not tonight?''

He smirked at the disappointment in her voice. ''I'm playing hockey tonight, but I'd love to have you in the stands rooting for me, if you'd like to come.''

''And after the hockey game...?'' She let her sentence trail off.

His grin widened. ''I'll take you to the B&B.''

''Couldn't we go back to your place afterward?''

"No way." He shook his head.

"Why not?"

"Because I'm clearing my calendar on Wednesday night for you. What I've got in mind, sweetheart, is going to take hours and hours and hours." And with that, he winked, chucked her under the chin, pivoted on his heel and strode out of the restaurant.

THE TEN PLAYERS whizzed over the ice in a blur. Hockey sticks clashed loudly in the still night air. Bright stadium lights lit the perimeter of the frozen lake turned outdoor hockey rink. In the bleachers, Kay sat huddled under a blanket with Jim and Linda Scofield, her notebook and pen clutched in her gloved fingers. She had yet to write a word, so caught up was she in watching the game.

The players zipped by them again heading for the opposite team's goal. If Quinn wasn't so tall, Kay would have had trouble following him. He moved with a graceful power, pushing across the ice with smooth, long-limbed strokes. The expression on his face showed fierce concentration. He manned his stick like a gladiator doing battle.

Wow. Did he bring that kind of concentration to the bedroom? Kay shivered at the thought, grateful she had the cold as an excuse for her quivers.

She was so busy eyeing Quinn's amazing bod, she never even noticed when he slammed the puck home until the crowd roared and jumped to their collective feet. Kay followed suit, dropping her notepad and pen into her seat so she could applaud without hindrance. "We Will Rock You" blared from the outdoor speakers mounted on the lampposts.

Because of his goal, the Bear Creek Grizzlies had taken a 2 to 1 lead.

"Quinn, Quinn, Quinn," the crowd chanted.

He turned then and caught Kay's eye.

A chill of excitement shuddered through her.

He put his hand to his mouth and blew her a kiss.

Kay's heart fluttered and her belly went warm against the sudden adrenaline rush. Quinn skated down the middle of the ice alone, his stick raised over his head in victory, accepting his accolades, relishing his accomplishment with unabashed glee.

The man was truly magnificent.

A warrior, self-reliant and strong. He was brave and passionate and not the least bit hesitant about expressing what was going on in his head.

Oh! To be like that, instead of a repressed rich woman so alienated from her emotions she didn't know if she would ever find the approval she needed to release herself from her societal prison.

"Kay, dear, you're shivering, get back under the blanket." Quinn's mother smiled and held up the thick thermal cover, welcoming her beneath it.

Kay sat beside Linda, squashing her notebook and pen beneath her, but she didn't care. Quinn's mom tucked the blanket around her and snuggled close. It felt nice to be wrapped in this warm cocoon, to share body heat with Quinn's family.

In that sweet moment she experienced an amiable sense of kinship she had never felt with her own mother. Linda Scofield, she knew with sudden certainty, would never advise her to marry a man who cheated on her.

Why can't my mother be like this?

But Kay knew it was a ridiculous wish. Wishing her

mother was different was like wishing that she was five inches taller or had been born in Bear Creek.

"Here comes Meggie," Linda said. "Let's scoot down."

Kay looked up to see a woman about her own age picking her way through the stands. Unlike everyone else, who were clad in mackinaws, boots and woolen pants, Meggie wore an outfit more like Kay's own stylish attire.

Meggie possessed an open, honest face and an understated but totally natural prettiness that would serve her well into middle age and beyond. Her eyelashes were enhanced with mascara, her cheeks heightened with rouge. Flame-red lipstick adorned her mouth. Her jet-black hair was tucked up under a bright red and orange cap.

Just like Kay, she looked out of place among the locals. City girls in the Arctic wilderness. Kay felt an instant kinship with her.

Meggie greeted her parents, then plunked down beside Kay. "Hi." She slipped off a glove to shake Kay's hand, revealing slender hands with short-trimmed but well-manicured nails. "I'm Meggie Drummond." Her lively green eyes twinkled. "And you must be Kay."

Kay nodded. "Nice to meet you," she said.

"I hear you're from New York City."

"Yes, I am."

"Wow, I've always wanted to go to New York. They practice some of the most cutting-edge medicine in the country."

"That's right, you're in the medical profession."

"Head nurse of the emergency department at Seattle Children's Hospital."

"Aren't you awfully young to be head nurse?"

Meggie grinned. "I live and breathe pediatric medicine."

"How are they managing without you?" Kay asked.

"Probably very happily since I'm not there to keep them in line." Meggie laughed. "I'm known as something of a taskmaster among my crew. I strive to be fair, but I've got high standards when it comes to patient care."

"I can see that about you."

Meggie's eyes sparkled at the compliment. Obviously, she loved her work. "I had lots of vacation time accumulated—in fact my boss was threatening to lock me out of the hospital if I didn't take off—then when Mom broke her ankle and needed help around the house, I figured now was as good as any to get away."

The woman was so easy to talk to. Friendly, frank, uninhibited, with definite opinions about the world. Just like Quinn.

"I'm going for hot chocolate," Quinn's dad announced, getting to his feet and taking his wife's hand. "You ladies want anything?"

Meggie, Kay and Linda all said they wanted one, and Jim climbed down the bleachers. When he was gone, Meggie turned back to Kay. "Quinn's been unable to talk about anything but you since he came back from New York."

"Really?"

"You've impressed the hell out of him."

"He's a special guy," Kay replied, surprised at the sudden pressure pushing at her heart like champagne bubbles against a bottle cork.

"Yeah," Meggie murmured, "real special. Can't

say I'm too keen on this modern-day mail-order-bride concept he's instigated.''

''No?''

''Oh, Meggie,'' her mother said, ''give it a chance. You never know what might happen.''

Meggie shook her head. ''He's just going to get hurt.''

''You think so?'' Kay asked.

''Uh-huh. You wouldn't believe it by looking at him, but Quinn's pretty tenderhearted. When he loves, he loves deeply.''

''That's true,'' Linda added.

Don't worry, Kay longed to tell them but couldn't. *This thing between us is purely physical. He won't fall in love with me.*

''He needs an Alaskan wife,'' Meggie said. ''Someone who understands him and his love for this land. I'm afraid that all he's going to get for his advertising dollars is a gaggle of giggling bimbos who'll take him for a ride, then skedaddle out of here at the first sign of winter. Just like Heather did.''

''His ex-girlfriend.''

''He told you about her?''

''Now, honey, don't judge Heather,'' Linda interjected. ''She just couldn't get used to the quiet of Bear Creek. Besides, isn't criticizing Heather's reluctance to live in Alaska a little bit of the pot calling the kettle black?''

''Hey,'' Meggie said, ''I never pretended to want to stay in Alaska. Even though I happened to be born here, I'm a city girl through and through. I gotta have action.''

''Isn't that the truth.'' Linda rolled her eyes. ''I

swear you kicked like a mule to get out the entire last trimester of my pregnancy."

"I love the city, too," Kay said, happy to have found a kindred spirit in this land of ice and snow.

"Honey, you are *the* city."

"I don't understand what's so fascinating about people being crammed on top of each other and driving like maniacs. What's the attraction?" Linda shook her head.

"Stimulating conversation," Meggie said.

"Great parties," Kay added.

"Museums," Meggie popped off.

"Shopping!" Kay grinned.

"Symphonies."

"The theater."

"Terrific Chinese take-out delivered right to your door!" they cried in unison, stared in awe at each other, then burst out laughing.

Kay felt instant camaraderie with Meggie, and the feeling astonished her. She didn't make friends this readily. Ever. But they'd forged a connection. She knew by the merry gleam shining in Meggie's blue-green eyes. She possessed the same irresistible magnetic personality as her older brother.

"My daughter, the cosmopolitan gourmand." Linda smiled indulgently. "Who'd have thought it when she was spitting peas in my face at ten months?"

"Ah, Mom. If you'd just give Seattle a chance, you'd love it."

"Not as much as I love Bear Creek," Linda replied adamantly.

Kay had to admire their affectionate mother-daughter exchange. She felt another twinge of sadness that she and her own mother would never have this kind of relationship.

The crowd roared again. Kay's attention was drawn back to the ice rink. Quinn had scored a second goal.

The referee blew his whistle. Shook his head, made some kind of motion with his hands.

The crowd booed.

Quinn skated over to the ref and shouted in his face. The man shouted back.

"What's happening?" Kay leaned over to whisper to Meggie.

"Ref's claiming the shot was no good. Puck got caught in the crease."

Quinn argued. The ref balked. Quinn gestured at the goal. The ref crossed his arms over his chest, adamantly shook his head.

It was exciting to watch Quinn. He was so ardent in his beliefs, and he didn't avoid conflict. Kay, a confrontation avoider from way back, couldn't help but admire his courage.

"Uh-oh," Meggie said.

"What? What?"

"The referee's going to toss Quinn out if he doesn't let up."

"Will he back down?"

"Not if he thinks he's right."

Nervously Kay raised a hand to her mouth and realized she had been holding her breath. The other players rallied around, tried to get Quinn to accept the verdict. But nothing doing. When Quinn took a stance, he took a stance. There'd be no swaying him from his original position. She found that passionate quality in him both compelling and disturbing.

The ref blew his whistle and pointed for Quinn to

leave the rink. Quinn ripped off his helmet and threw it on the ice.

Kay's stomach looped and dived like she was on a roller-coaster ride.

''Yep,'' said outspoken Meggie. ''It's going to take more than some sweet little city girl from the lower forty-eight to corral our Quinn.''

8

"HI THERE, BEAUTIFUL," Quinn said when Kay came over to sit beside him. He was sitting on the sidelines unlacing his skates.

Happy to see her, he raked his gaze over her body. She looked stunning in that white ski-bunny suit with the hood zipped up around her head. To think she was here with him made his heart give this strange little hop.

She'd stood in the stands with his family and friends, looking like a pristine rose in a field of wild, black-eyed Susans, until Meggie had shown up. The appearance of those two city girls in Bear Creek added color to the place. He imagined the streets filled with pretty women, and his heart soared. That was exactly what the town needed to pump some life into it, and even if he personally didn't find a wife, if his ad pulled women into Bear Creek, then it was money well spent.

While he'd been playing hockey, he had tried hard not to look Kay's way too often, because every time he did he got distracted. An unusual occurrence. He found her power over him slightly disturbing.

Just hormones, pal. Don't read more into it than there is.

"Too bad about the ref's call." She nodded at the game still in progress.

"I was robbed." He grinned. "I made that shot fair and square. Where's instant replay when you need it?"

"Does it really matter? Your team is still in the lead."

He stared at her in disbelief. "Of course it matters. I was right."

"Yes, but your stubbornness got you thrown out of the game."

He shook his head. Was this discussion about much more than hockey? "Ah, your politically correct side rears its head."

"What's that supposed to mean?"

"Nothing. Forget I said anything."

"No. I want to know."

"You were raised in a world where you subjugated your beliefs in order to fit in with those around you."

"And you think that's bad?"

"I didn't say it was bad." He removed his skates, jammed his feet into his boots. "It's just not the way I was brought up. My folks taught me the most important things were honesty and integrity. If you're right and you know it, you don't buckle no matter what the peer pressure, and you don't care what others think about you as long as you know you've done the right thing."

"And arguing with the ref was the right thing to do?"

"Yes. He was wrong. I made that goal."

"And if you'd been mistaken?"

"I'd swallow my pride and admit it."

She looked at him a long moment. A peculiar queasiness assailed him. Had he put her off by being himself? But hell, he didn't know any other way to be. He couldn't pretend to be something he wasn't. He hadn't been schooled in subterfuge the way she obviously had. He wasn't well versed in suppressing his convictions. Nor did he want to be.

"It's my opinion that nothing important was ever gained by sitting back and keeping your mouth shut," he expounded. "If you have something important to say, say it. If you don't let people know what's on your mind, how are they ever going to understand you?"

Kay shrugged. "Is it important for everyone to understand you?"

"Not everyone, no. But the people you care about, the people you deal with on a daily basis."

"I'm not sure I agree with that."

"Fair enough. You're entitled to your opinions, just as I am to mine."

"I think one can say too much and change a good impression into a bad one."

"But if you're just letting people know who you are, where you're coming from, then how can that be a mistake? If they dislike you for what you believe in, then they dislike you. If they admire you simply for the image you portray, then how do people ever get to know the real you?"

Kay said nothing at all. Instead, she studied him silently.

"Like now. You're thinking I'm full of crap, but you're too polite to tell me to go take a flying leap. Right?"

"What gave you that idea?'

"Right?" He cocked his head, gave her his most dazzling grin.

She smiled then, a little sheepishly. "Okay. All right. Yes, I do think you're full of it."

He pushed to his feet, threw an arm around her shoulders, drew her close to his body. "See there, sweetheart? That wasn't so hard, was it?"

"Not too hard," she admitted.

"Come on." He chucked her under the chin. "I'll take you back to Jake's."

She gave him her hand, and he knew then that everything was okay between them. She accepted him for who he was. Her approval lifted his spirits, and his feelings for her took on a new dimension. They could disagree and still respect each other.

He kissed her under the porch light of Jake's establishment. He knew full well that half the town was peering through their curtains watching them, but he didn't care. Let 'em gawk.

A groan escaped his throat and he tugged her flush against the length of him. She kept her eyes wide open during the kiss and so did he. Damn, but it was erotic. They couldn't seem to peer deeply enough into each other. Her pupils dilated and her lips softened.

She tasted ripe, willing, ready. He couldn't wait for tomorrow night. Couldn't wait to see how she responded to the things he had in store for her.

Pulling away, he stroked her jawline with his thumb. "I wish I knew all the thoughts that passed through that magnificent brain of yours. I wish I could know the real Kay Freemont."

"That'd be quite a trick," she said huskily, "since I'm not sure I even know myself."

The weird thing was, Kay already felt as if he *could* read her mind at times, and she couldn't figure out where he'd obtained this amazing ability. Why was this man so different from any other she had ever known? She'd heard that men were supposed to hate talking about things like feelings and emotions and sentiment. Especially masculine men of action like this one.

"Please," he encouraged, his eyes softening, his pupils dilating, "talk to me. Let me in. I'm dying to know everything there is to know about you. What are your hopes, your dreams, your wishes?"

She realized then that he wasn't this inquisitive with all women, that it was she alone who interested him. The thought terrified her. "I'm wishing you would kiss me again."

"I think you're evading my questions, but that's a wish I can't pass by." Quinn smiled so deeply he felt the edges of his eyelids crinkle, and he leaned in to take her lips once more.

She was like velvet heat in his mouth.

He thought of hot-fudge sundaes and chocolate fondue and cinnamon rolls drizzled with melted butter.

Then, irrationally, he thought of all the things he wanted to do with her that he never could. Necking in the balcony of a sexy, romantic movie. Holding hands and ice-skating on a frozen pond. Sharing a banana split and listening to fifties music on a jukebox at Marilyn Hecate's soda fountain in July. With Kay, he wanted to be a kid again, exploring her with the eager enthusiasm of a seventeen-year-old in the back seat of his daddy's car.

What would she think if he told her all this? Would he chase her away with his honesty?

He cupped her firm yet soft fanny with one hand,

but the excess padding of her ski suit frustrated him. His fingers ached to glide over her bare skin. His hands cried out to knead her tender flesh. His palm itched to delve into new and exciting places.

Her scent filled his nose. That lovely aroma of jasmine mingled with her own natural windswept smell, and his knees loosened. He wanted to lay her down on the sidewalk and do all kinds of decadent things to her.

"I can't wait until tomorrow," she murmured into his mouth expressing exactly what was on his mind.

"Me, neither." His voice was gruff and his body had gone rigid from the taste of her. The chase was on. His hunter's instincts were roused. His sporting blood boiled.

"Will we be doing more aurora-gazing?"

"No, I've got something else in mind."

"Oh?" He heard the excitement in her voice and it served to supercharge his erection.

"Yeah." He grinned. "I'll pick you up at five-thirty. But be forewarned. You might want to bring a change of clothes."

HIS CRYPTIC WORDS had sent her into orbit.

What in the heck did he mean? Kay wondered as she rifled through the clothes she had brought with her, excitement racing up her nerve endings until she tingled with heightened anticipation. Had he known what effect his statement would have on her? Driving her crazy with curiosity.

The man was a genius at mind games.

After much deliberation, she dressed simply in black jeans and a sapphire turtleneck sweater, then stashed a pair of woolen slacks and a crimson blouse into her satchel. As she was applying the finishing touches to her makeup, the telephone rang.

"Hello?"

"How's the article coming?"

Kay winced. Judy.

"I was just getting ready for bed and thought I'd give you a call. Is that hunky bachelor keeping you warm on those cold winter nights?"

"Oh, please."

"Go ahead, lie to me if you want to, darling, but don't lie to yourself. Any fool can see there's chemistry between you two. I'm not going to lose my prize reporter to the Alaskan wilderness, am I?"

"Don't be ridiculous, Judy. I'm not about to stay in Alaska. It's dark nearly twenty hours a day."

"I don't know. That Quinn is pretty cute. You're never going to find anyone like him in Manhattan."

"And it's freezing cold. I have to wear three layers of clothing to stay comfortable, even indoors. Hard to get romantic under those conditions."

Then again there was nothing more romantic than body heat.

"So if you're not canoodling with bachelor number one, where were you last night when I tried to call?"

Sampling a taste of heaven.

"Out doing research."

It wasn't a lie. She had been researching Quinn's background for the article, never mind that her research had concluded with some fierce kissing.

Judy didn't need the details. She had nothing to worry about. Once Kay returned to New York a satisfied woman, she would never see Quinn again.

Why that thought made her tummy ache, she couldn't say.

"I hope you got some good info."

Oh, it was good all right. Sinfully good. The best. And just as soon as Judy hung up the phone, she was going back for seconds.

BLUSTERER. BLUFFER. Blowhard.

Quinn had shot off his mouth and told Kay he was capable of giving her an orgasm. Now that she was sitting here in his kitchen and the moment was at hand, he was panicking.

Big time.

What if he failed her?

Over the course of his thirty-two years, he'd satisfied many lovers. Several of his former girlfriends had affectionately dubbed him Slow Hand. He loved making love and he loved pleasuring his partner.

But this was different. This was pressure. Kay's whole sexual awakening lay in his hands, and his normal cockiness had deserted him. Especially because that dynamite body of hers drove him to distraction.

Quinn refused to be like the other men of her acquaintance. He refused to let her down, and he intended on devoting himself to the pursuit of her orgasm while putting his own needs on hold. Because that was what she deserved.

Kay was exceptional.

Would ten days with her be enough for him? After Kay, would any woman be enough?

Don't get all romantic, Scofield, he told himself. *This is only sex and you know it. You're getting mixed up because you want to get married. But let's get real for a moment. You could never provide a woman like Kay with the things she needs. She's accustomed to bright lights and the big city.* It was honor enough that she had selected him as her sexual teacher. He took his responsibility seriously. He wouldn't ask for more than she could give.

Kay cleared her throat and he realized several minutes had passed where he'd done little more than stare at her when he was supposed to be making them a cup of hot tea.

"So." She rubbed her palms together, and that was when he realized she was as nervous as he. "So when do we begin?"

Virgins on their wedding night couldn't have been more unstrung.

He took a step toward her, his heart pounding. Damn, but she was breathtaking. She practically glowed, her features arranged in a piquant orchestration of enthusiasm and excitement.

Gone was her normally reserved demeanor. Her mahogany eyes had a fervent gleam. Her mouth was tipped up in a zealous grin. Her brightness, sunny as the twenty-four-hour summer solstice in the Arctic circle, completely bowled him over.

You're the man. The one with the supposed experience in eliciting women's orgasms. Take charge. Do something, dillweed.

But he couldn't do more than stare at her. "You look beautiful," he said.

"Thank you." She ducked her head.

This wouldn't do. Casanova didn't win women with clichéd compliments and an "aw shucks" attitude.

"Well," she asked, sneaking a surreptitious glance at his face, "what's the first lesson?"

"We're going back to the basics," he said, her question unfreezing him at last.

"The basics?"

"Don't ask questions." He reached out a hand to her. "Come here."

And damn, if she didn't giggle just a little bit as she slipped off the bar stool and placed her small, soft hand in his. He would have thought such an elegant woman incapable of giggling. He also never thought a giggle could have such a profound effect him.

"Did you bring a change of clothes?" he asked.

"Yes, and that's been driving me crazy all day. Why did I need a change of clothes?"

"Shh. No questions, remember. I want you to sit here." He patted the tabletop.

"On the table?"

"Was that a question?"

"My mother would have a fit if she caught me sitting on the table."

"All the more reason to sit there."

"You're sure this is necessary?"

"No questions," he growled, feigning sternness.

She clapped her hand over her mouth. "Oops, forgot. Questions, curse of the journalist. I'm sorry."

Without warning, he cupped her under the chin with his fingers and forced her gaze upward so she had no choice but to look him squarely in the face. Her eyes were so deep and brown and inquisitive he immediately felt as if he were drowning in a vat of chocolate.

"Trust me." He could tell this was difficult for her, letting go of control, trusting a man she didn't know very well. But that was exactly why it was so important for her to do it.

"Okay." She nodded in agreement, her expression softening. He was stunned by how much she wanted this. Even enough to go against her instincts.

He put his hands around her slender waist and lifted her onto the table. He could see her pulse racing in the hollow of her throat, and the intoxicating sight caused him to stiffen again.

She watched him as he drew the silk tie from his pocket. Her breathing quickened, grew shallower as he slowly ran his hands over the delicate material until he had one end clutched in each fist.

The tip of her tongue flicked out to moisten her lips. A glimmer of expectation lit her eyes.

She looked from the tie to his face and back again. She swallowed hard.

"I want to ask a question."

"No."

She clenched her jaw. He saw the muscles work beneath her skin.

"You want to know what I'm going to do with this tie. Is that correct?"

She nodded.

"I'm going deprive you of the sense of sight."

Kay gulped and a tremor passed through her at the wolfish expression in Quinn's eyes, at the unmistakable feral intent…but she wasn't scared. Instead, she was very turned on and extremely aware of her body's heated response—the reckless stagger of her pulse, the incandescent spark that shot through her veins and rooted low in her belly, the sudden dryness in her palms and equally sudden moistness in her most feminine place.

He approached like a lion stalking his prey. Leaning forward, his chest bumped into hers as he secured the tie around her eyes. Her nipples hardened in instant response. How she wished they were naked, with his bare, muscled chest pushed against them.

He secured the tie, cutting off her vision.

Blind. Sightless. And questionless, too. She couldn't even ask him why he was doing the things he was doing to her. She was at his mercy.

A spark of fear touched her then. Fear and an accompanying thrill. Trust was not her strong suit. She had resided too long in New York. Lived too many years as a Freemont woman. She wasn't like the Alaskans she'd met, who'd assumed everyone was a friend until proved otherwise.

But she had asked for his help, and he was giving it to her. Too late to back out.

Quinn pressed something into her hand. Her fingers closed around it. She recognized the shape. A metal whistle on a chain.

"Now," he said, "if you start to feel uncomfortable with anything that happens, I want you to blow this whistle. I'll stop immediately. But I ask you to bear with me and give it a chance before you resort to the whistle. Once the whistle blows, the evening is over. Understand?"

She nodded, comforted that he'd given her a way out, but determined not to use the whistle, no matter what.

He took the whistle and slipped the chain around

her neck. ''We start,'' he said, ''with the sense of taste.''

Her tongue responded to his suggestion. It began to tingle and her mouth watered. She realized her entire body was tensed. Waiting.

She felt him move away from the table, heard the oven door open. Her nose twitched at the bewitching scents. The spicy aroma of barbecue, she recognized. And was that fried chicken?

His footsteps sounded on the hardwood floor as he tromped back over to her. His finger touched her chin, and she parted her bottom lip.

''What is this?'' he asked.

She bit into the morsel he offered. ''Barbecued ribs.''

''No, go deeper,'' he insisted. ''What does it taste like?''

She frowned. ''I don't understand.''

''Dig, Kay.''

She felt the pressure of his hand on her knees. Sighing with exasperation, she said, ''Pork. It tastes like pork ribs.''

''I can see why you have so much trouble with sex. You're too literal in your thinking.''

''Frankly,'' she said, a little annoyed with him, ''I don't see what this has to do with sex.''

''That's your problem, sweetheart, but don't worry. Quinn's here to help.''

She was about to tell him he was acting like a pompous ass when she felt a flutter as his lips brushed her throat. Spicy sparks shot through her system. Okay, maybe she was wrong and he was right about this.

"This is your reward," he said huskily. "Answer my questions and you get more kisses."

"Tangy," she said. "Rich. Full. Smoky. Woodsy. Oaken."

"Yes, ma'am, I'm impressed. See what you can do when you put your mind to it?"

What a heavenly assault! Her senses sung to life and she was aware of everything not visual. Quinn's musky male smell. The scent of spray starch on his shirt. The pressure of his hand on her shoulder. The hardness of the table beneath her bottom. The flavor of barbecue lingering on her tongue. The faint plunk-plunk-plunk of water droplets from a leaky faucet hitting the bottom of the stainless-steel sink.

From head to toe, her body tingled. Tingled and prickled and quivered.

He pressed something else to her lips. An icy coldness that was a brisk contrast to the warmth of his fingers.

"Ice cube," she said as he traced her mouth with it. "Cold. Frosty. Tasteless."

"Stick out your tongue."

She extended her tongue. He dropped the ice cube onto it.

"Now suck."

She wrapped her tongue around the ice cube, sucked gently as it melted.

"What does it taste like?"

"No taste."

"Wrong. Try again. Use your imagination. You're a writer—I know you've got one."

"It tastes like winter."

"More."

"Refreshing. Invigorating. Chilling."

"I'm very proud of you." He rewarded her with a rain of kisses, showering her forehead, the tip of her nose, her cheeks and chin.

She thrilled to his kisses, exalted in having earned them. She had pleased him. This sensory deprivation was driving her mad. She wanted to rip the tie off so she could see his face, gaze deeply into his eyes.

She reached to undo the tie, but he saw her intent and stilled her hand.

"Oh, no, sweetheart. There's much more to do. The night is young and we've only just begun."

He fed her more tidbits and made her describe each one in detail. She got into the spirit of the game, and when he gave her salsa guacamole in corn tortillas she exclaimed, "Lime, tequila, sangria, Acapulco sunsets, hot sand, thong bikinis."

When he handed her a slick, round cob of corn, she bit into it and pronounced, "Crunchy, buttery, hot, salty. Summer. Fireflies. Picnic tables."

He pushed the sleeve of her sweater to just above the elbow and slowly kissed and nibbled a blazing path up her arm.

"Ah," he said. "I think I've made my point. We move on to the next phase."

"You're a wicked man, Quinn Scofield, to torture me so."

He chuckled. The fertile sound resonated in her ears. She could tell so much from his laughter. She heard passion and kindness, humor and an earthy intelligence.

"Come."

His fingers reached for hers and he helped her slide

off the table. Her feet touched the floor and she realized she was eye level with his chin. She knew her face was decorated with barbecue sauce and corn nibbles and smears of guacamole. She felt like a messy kid.

She reached out a hand to touch him and he stood perfectly still and allowed her to run her fingers over his features the way a blind person might.

Her fingers trailed over to his nose. A sturdy masculine nose that was neither too large or too small, but bent slightly, knocked crooked from playing one too many games of hockey.

From his nose, her fingertips migrated to his mouth. Oh, this was dangerous territory. Firm and wide. Hearty and willing. His lips parted and he licked lightly at her fingertips, sending a blast of high-voltage electricity coursing through her body.

Startled, she jerked her hand away.

He laughed again, delighted with her, and began to clean her with big, wet kisses. His tongue frolicked over her upper lip.

"Mmm," he said. "You've never lived until you've slurped barbecue off the face of a beautiful woman."

"I think I'll trust you on that one." She laughed. "What's next?"

"Dessert, and in the process, we're going to fully explore the sense of touch."

"Oh." She inhaled sharply.

His hand reached for the button on her sweater. She stiffened beside him.

"Relax," he soothed. "We've got to get you out of these messy clothes. Take a long, slow, deep breath."

She obeyed. What else could she do? She wanted

this so much. And yet she felt vulnerable, standing here blindfolded while he got to watch her every move.

Button by button, he undid her sweater, then carefully slid her arms from the sleeves.

He hissed in a breath.

"What?" she asked, then remembered she wasn't supposed to ask questions.

But this time he answered her. "That black lace bra. It's giving me a hard-on that won't quit."

Heat spread from her neck to her face. Blushing, the scourge of the blonde.

"Any woman who wears the kind of lingerie you wear can't be frigid. You've just been waiting for someone to treasure you."

To Kay's horror, she began to cry. Fortunately, she had on the blindfold.

9

"WHAT'S WRONG?" Quinn asked. He drew her to him, her naked skin pressed against the crispness of his shirt, the metal whistle imprinted below the hollow of her throat. "Did I say something to offend you?"

She shook her head.

"I shouldn't have made that crack about my hard-on. I just wanted you to know how much you move me."

"It wasn't that remark." She sniffled. "I'm a New Yorker, after all. I hear much worse than that on my walk to work."

"What is it, then?" He sounded genuinely worried, and his tenderness only exacerbated her emotions.

"No one's ever treasured me before." She placed a palm to her mouth and tried to will herself to stop crying.

Her feet left the floor when he clasped her so tightly she could hear the steady lub-dub of his heart. "I know, baby, I know."

And then he just held her for the longest moment.

"Maybe we should call it a night," he said, gently easing her back down to the floor. "I didn't mean to upset you."

"No," she said. "I want to continue."

"Are you sure?"

She nodded, and imagined she looked pretty incongruous standing there in a blindfold, black lace bra and her black denim jeans.

"I wasn't going to do this yet, but I can't help myself." The next thing she knew he was on his knees in front of her kissing her belly and easing down the zipper on her jeans.

Kay caught her breath. So this was it. They were going to make love on the kitchen floor. Couldn't get much wilder than that. She thought back on some of the articles she had written for *Metropolitan.* Articles on spontaneity. Well, for once she was about to practice what she preached.

Once her pants were undone, Quinn placed a hand on either side of her and slowly began to nudge the thick material down over the curve of her hips.

"More sexy underwear." He groaned when he spied her black thong. "You're going to propel me over the brink, woman."

His comment filled her with elation. She liked that she had the power to literally bring him to his knees. She had never held such control over Lloyd. He had acted as if her body was nothing special. In fact, he often prodded her to lose weight, and for heaven's sake, at five-five she only weighed 115 pounds.

But Quinn seemed to relish her curves, and his appreciation made her feel like a goddess.

"Step out of your pants," he instructed when he'd pooled the material around her ankles.

Trembling, she did as he asked. She still wore her boots and her underwear. Would he make love to her with her boots on? She found the thought incredibly erotic.

What now? What would come next? Her mind sprinted ahead of her body, imagining them coiled in the throes of sex, the hardwood floor pressing into her back.

But then he surprised her yet again by taking her hand and leading her through the house.

"I'm going to push you right to the edge," he growled in her ear, "and then pull you back before you tumble over."

She gasped, heard him open a door and felt a gust of frigid air. He was taking her outside!

He opened another door and a moist, heated blast washed over her. She smelled cedar and dampness. He closed the door behind them.

"My sauna." He directed her to sit on a bench.

Her skin came alive. It seemed separate from the rest of her, as if it were a living, breathing organism all its own. Goose bumps piled up. Everything she touched was greatly magnified. The rough feel of the cedar bench, the damp heat draping over her body, the soft silk of the tie binding her eyes.

"I'll be right back with dessert," he whispered, his lips on her ear. "Don't go anywhere."

She sat in total silence for a moment, soaking in the experience, reassuring herself that this was indeed happening to her, that she wasn't caught in the sleepy midst of one of her explosive fantasies.

The door snapped open again. Quinn pressed something into her hand. "For you."

Her fingers were wrapped around an ice-cream cone. Kay laughed. Ice cream in a sauna?

"Hold mine a minute." He handed her a second cone and stepped away from her.

Her ears, attuned to the slightest nuance in sound, pricked up when she heard the whisper of material and realized he was getting undressed. Not being able to see him catapulted her excitement into overdrive, and she found herself growing hotter and wetter than the sauna itself. When he finally settled himself on the bench beside her, it seemed as if her heart had ceased beating.

Waiting.

Perspiration pearled around her collarbones, trickled down her chest. The silence was deafening.

"Thanks for holding my cone."

He took it from her. By now, her ice cream was melting in a sticky stream down her wrist.

"Oops," he said. "Let me lick that off for you."

He flicked his tongue around her wrist and Kay groaned. Then she felt something cold plop onto her breast.

"Sorry, lost the top of my cone."

Then his tongue was on her skin just above her cleavage, and he was licking with mad abandon.

"Gotta eat it all up before it melts," he gasped.

He went back and forth in rapid motion, first feasting at her breasts, then sucking on her gooey fingers. Kay was mad with the sensation of his hot, wet, sticky tongue seemingly everywhere at the same time. She dropped her cone. It hit the floor with a soft crunch, but she didn't care. She was drowning, falling, dripping into a pool of crazy agitation.

"I want a taste!" she cried.

So he kissed her on the lips, his mouth full of ice cream.

"Mmm, chocolate," she cooed. "No wait—vanilla? Strawberry?"

"Neopolitan."

"Ah. That explains the mix of flavors."

His gooey hands were on her shoulders, then her

stomach. Damn this blindfold! She wanted to see him, wanted to watch what he was doing with that awesome tongue.

But then he stopped licking.

"What's wrong?" she whimpered.

"Damn," he said, disappointment winding through the timbre of his voice. "The ice cream is all gone, and we're running out of steam."

Quinn shifted off the bench, and she heard the sound of water being poured over the hot lava rocks. Hiss. Sizzle. Fresh steam rose and rolled over her skin, muggy as summertime in New Orleans. He returned to his seat beside her but said nothing.

Kay waited.

And tried to imagine what he looked like naked.

She wanted to ask what they were waiting for, but he'd warned her not to ask questions, and she was determined to play the game his way.

Finally she couldn't stand the tension any longer. She reached out. Her hand collided with his forearm. Ah, those forearms that stoked an instant flame inside her. She wrapped her fingers around his wrist, crushed his arm hairs now damp with humidity beneath the palm of her hand.

"Quinn, I want you," she whispered.

"Then come here."

He took her by the waist and lifted her onto his naked lap. She straddled him, his incredibly hard erection caught between their naked bellies.

"Oh!" she exclaimed because she could not think of one single thing to say to express her feelings. "Oh."

"See what you do to me, woman?" He leaned close to growl in her ear.

Quinn cupped the sweet curve of her lush bottom left exposed by those dental-floss-size panties and pulled her even closer.

She made a little noise, soft and low, and the sound drilled a hole straight through his gut. She settled her hands on his shoulders. Her lovely breasts overflowed the lace of her low-cut bra. Like flags of pink velvet, her jaunty nipples peeked out above the delicate fabric gone soggy from the sauna.

Quinn wanted to seize her right then and there. Wanted to lower her onto his throbbing shaft and give her the ride of her life.

Control, he warned himself. This night was about Kay's pleasure, not his own. He was going to drag this out as long as humanly possible. He was helping her explore her erogenous zones so that when she did finally climax, it would be like scaling Mount Everest, thrilling, incomparable, the experience of a lifetime and thoroughly earned.

Damn, but he should have spent some private time in the shower before he picked her up. Mentally steeling himself against the growing pressure inside him, Quinn dipped his head and suckled first one perky nipple and then the other.

Her fingers flew to his hair and knotted there as if she was anchoring herself in place. She wriggled and squirmed and writhed against him.

"Experience this with your skin," he instructed in a voice choked with lust. "Focus on what you're feeling. Tell me about it."

"Hot," she gasped. "Utterly hot."

"And?"

"Wet and slick and slippery."

"More."

''Mucky, sticky, spongy.''

''Yes.''

''Squishy, sloppy, soggy.''

''Don't stop.''

''Pervaded, persuaded, invaded.''

''Go, go.''

''Drenched, saturated, undone.'' She was breathing heavily, her breasts rising and falling with each ragged pant. The tail end of the tie, soaked with steam and perspiration, trailed down her slender shoulders.

''Burning!'' she cried. ''Sweating, sweltering, ablaze.''

A strand of hair was plastered to her forehead. He would never have believed the cool, sophisticated woman he'd met at the offices of *Metropolitan* magazine could be so completely wanton. And so totally delicious.

Quinn loved it.

Man alive, how he loved it.

He had to grit his teeth and clench his fists to keep from tearing off that scrap of panty and piercing her through with his pulsating sword. The instinct to sheathe himself deep inside her was primitive. If he didn't get her out of here quickly, he'd mangle everything he was building toward.

''Let's go,'' he said.

''Wh...what?'' She bobbed her head at him, raised a hand to her tie.

''Leave it.''

''I don't understand.''

''Hush.'' He tugged her off his lap, her booted feet bumping lightly into his shins.

''But Quinn...'' she protested.

He didn't give her a chance; he just dragged her

from the sauna and plunged them, steam rising from their bodies, into the cold, cold night. The air was brisk, the northern sky filled with dancing light. Quinn realized with a start that Kay wasn't the only one having her senses put through the paces. The moment seemed utterly surreal. Like something from an erotic fantasy poem.

Holding hands, they ran together through the snow. He pulled up short beside the house and leaped with her into a snowbank.

"Omigosh!" Kay exclaimed. "This is absolutely exhilarating. Like a splash of cold water on a muggy August afternoon in Manhattan."

Her skin had pinked, her cheeks flushed red. A huge grin decorated her face, and the sight of her joy tugged at Quinn's heartstrings.

Watch out, Scofield! You're treading on thin ice here. She's not available. She's on the rebound.

"I'm floored," Kay said, apparently invigorated by the experience. "Completely floored."

"Enough," Quinn said. "We don't want to get frostbite."

"How could you get frostbite from something that feels so lovely?"

"Trust me on this." He struggled to his feet, his arousal gone, and reached down to help her from the snowbank.

"You're amazing," she said.

"Me?" He speared her with his eyes, raked his gaze over her body. "I don't think so."

She wagged a finger at him. "Oh, yes, you are."

"Let's get you inside, Miss Eskimo. I'm beginning to think the cold has gone to your head." Feeling inexplicably protective, he placed a hand to her back and swept her up the walk beside him.

She was shivering so hard her teeth were clattering by the time he got her to the fireplace. He wrapped her snugly in a quilt and seated her on the hearth. "Don't move," he said. "I'll be right back with a hot toddy."

Before going to the kitchen, he hurried to his bedroom and pulled on red nylon jogging shorts and a T-shirt that said, "Mountain Climbers Never Die, They Just Reach Their Peak." He wasn't cold; he did the sauna-snowbank thing on a regular basis, but he didn't want Kay to see him naked. Not yet.

A few minutes later he settled a mug of Irish coffee in her hands and untied the blindfold.

She blinked up at him, the firelight reflecting the golden strands of her disheveled hair. Her mascara had smeared a little, causing her eyes to look wide despite their slightly almond shape.

He liked her like this, Quinn realized. Mussed and rumpled and smiling. Bang, bang, bang, went his heart.

"What?" she asked. "Or am I still not allowed to ask questions?"

"Game over," he said. "And I was just shaking my head in amazement at how beautiful you are."

She raised a hand to her head. "Yuck! My hair's all clumpy with melted ice cream. I must look like a bachelor pad at 4 a.m. on New Year's Day."

He sat beside her, stared into her eyes. "You don't need hairspray and makeup and fancy creams to look beautiful, Kay."

"Ha! Tell that to my mother. She'd be appalled if she could see me now. Appalled on so many levels."

"You've spent your life trying to please your parents."

"Well, that's part of why I'm here. To start untying those apron strings."

"I'm your bit of rebellion."

"Kind of," she admitted.

He'd suspected as much, and he shouldn't have been surprised or even disappointed by the knowledge. But he couldn't help but wish that she'd come to Alaska because she liked him, not to piss off her parents or learn how to exceed her sexual speed limit.

Still, she was here and he wanted her, and he certainly wasn't going to send her away. She would be a sweet memory. His time with Kay was teaching him more and more what it was he wanted from a wife. Maybe that was the whole cosmic reason of their meeting in the first place.

He realized he needed someone more like him. Someone with the same traditional family values, the same kind of experiences, the same love of the land, the same frank ability to speak her mind. He tried to imagine Kay living in Alaska and failed completely. She would survive here about as well as a hothouse orchid.

"So what happens next?" she asked.

"Clean up," he said as they moved to the bathroom. "You're gonna love this."

"Should I take off my underwear?"

She was glad to have the blindfold removed, glad to be able to see him. He was wearing a pair of jogging shorts, but there was no hiding the imposing package that bulged beneath the constricting material.

"Get in the shower." He tested the temperature with his forearm. "Just as you are."

"Aren't you getting in, too?"

"Right behind you, sweetheart."

Giddily she stepped into the warm shower. He climbed in beside her and pulled the glass shower door closed. He took her in his arms and smothered her giggles with kisses. She felt as if she was eighteen again and experiencing sexual pleasure for the very first time.

Ah, this was what she wanted. This was why she had come to Alaska. To wipe her sexual slate clean and start fresh.

He reached around her for the bath gel and squirted a dollop into the palm of his hand. The almost empty bottle made a wheezing noise that had her giggling again. He began lathering her up, scrubbing her through her saturated underclothes.

The sensation of his warm, slippery skin massaging her through wet lace was intensely erotic. His hand slid over her smooth mound, and her slick, soapy panties pulled against the curve of her buttocks and plucked tightly over her most feminine and sensitive flesh.

Kay closed her eyes and clung to him. With one hand, he stroked a swollen breast through her bra.

He was a master of exquisite torture.

The steam, the sensuous spray of warm water, the stimulation of his wet fingers were more than she could tolerate. He deserved to get a healthy serving of what he was dishing up.

She smiled devilishly and reached for him.

Quinn gulped. The woman was turning the tables on him. Didn't she realize how truly dangerous that was? If she wanted her longed-for orgasm, she'd better stop rubbing him down there.

Leaning into him, she nuzzled up hard against his chest. Right then and there he knew he wasn't as in charge of the situation as he wanted to be. She kissed him then, sinking her fingers into his shoulders to hold him still.

The force of her kiss surprised him and stoked his own internal furnace higher and hotter. She made sweet mewling sounds deep in her throat.

He felt like a fallen mountain climber, dangling precariously from the end of a taut rescue line. Every muscle in his body tensed. His erection was so damned hard he feared he'd turned to granite, and he yearned for her with a desperate urgency that scared the hell out of him.

Ah, he was lost!

"Don't stop," she whimpered. "More, more."

He clutched her hips and ground himself against her far more roughly than he'd intended. The thin material of her thong rubbed provocatively against his nylon jogging shorts, and he about flipped.

"Yes, Quinn, now!" she cried, and pressed her breasts so tightly to his chest that the whistle around her neck made an indention in his skin. The whistle he'd given her to blow if things got too out of hand. "Make love to me right here in the shower. I'm ready."

He was startled to discover she welcomed his aggressiveness. His lack of control hadn't scared her one bit.

But it scared him.

Desperately Quinn reached for the whistle, took it from around her neck, pressed the wet metal tightly against his lips and blew.

10

WHEN HE ARRIVED on Friday evening to escort Kay to his parents' dinner party, Quinn didn't say a word about what had happened between them. But he did take her arm possessively. He angled her a glance that made her feel all woman. She was ready to skip the party and head back to his place for another love lesson.

Since Wednesday night, she had been unable to think of anything but Quinn. To hell with the article. To hell with work. She caught herself lying on the bed at the bed-and-breakfast staring at the ceiling and recalling ever nuance of what they'd shared. And she imagined what other wicked treats he had up his sleeve.

The Scofields' large, homey kitchen was crowded with Quinn's laughing family and friends. The decor was an eclectic hodgepodge. Nothing looked as if it fit. Just like at Quinn's place, his parents had rafter ceilings and leather furniture.

A stenciled border featuring moose and bear and salmon ran along the kitchen wall. A carved totem pole in the corner did double duty as a coatrack. Numerous knickknacks graced shelves and corner nooks. Photographs of Quinn and Meggie as children graced the walls. Gingham curtains hung in the kitchen window. Slightly bawdy cartoons were stuck with magnets to the refrigerator. A pot of plastic flowers on the window ledge sang "Let the Sunshine In" and twirled wildly in opposite directions when anyone approached.

Honoria would have blanched at the sight and proclaimed the house "irreparably tacky." Kay found the place both charming and comfortable. It was a real home, not a museum showcase like her parents' penthouse apartment in Manhattan or their summer retreat in the Hamptons.

The smell of sourdough bread and beef stew permeated the room. Everyone was milling around, talking at once, balancing hearty bowls of stew and slabs of buttered bread in their hands. Raucous classic rock music underscored the gathering. Jim Scofield filled his guests' mugs full of frothy ale from a tapped keg. In the next room a lively group of poker players yelled good-natured insults at one another.

Kay had never witnessed anything like this jolly free-for-all at her parents' parties, where guests nibbled exotic tidbits from silver trays and sedate classical music poured through the piped-in system.

At first she had been taken aback by the exuberant rowdiness. But when she thought about how her mother would have turned up her nose at such a party, she began to relax and enjoy the camaraderie. She was here to experience Alaska as it was—sprawling, unruly, wildly independent—not to resort to prejudices against what Honoria would call "common folk."

Even though she had become unhappy with things of late, Kay had never really realized how much she'd lived in an ivory tower or how cruelly snobbish her family was. This new knowledge reinforced her desire to become more open, more accepting, more forgiving of others.

All four bachelors were in attendance at the party. In fact, the house was crowded with men. Kay and Meggie were the only single women under thirty-five. In fact, they were the *only* women under thirty-five except for six-months-pregnant Candy Kilstrom, wife of KCRK disk jockey, Liam.

Quickly enough Kay learned that Jake was the life of the party, cracking jokes and telling stories. He possessed a keen wit and grinned ninety percent of the time.

Mack, the shortest of the bachelors but by no means small, never seemed to stop moving. He was quick and industrious, the first to volunteer when Quinn's father had asked for help unloading the keg.

Caleb was hard to figure. His calm nature drew her, but he didn't say much and preferred to stay perched in the corner watching the others with a sage smile. She did notice that whenever he glanced at Meggie, his smile disappeared and his dark eyes turned moody and restless. Kay wondered if he disliked the young woman for some reason.

If that was the case, she didn't know why. Kay really liked the straightforward woman, who seemed to have the courage to say all the things Kay thought but wasn't candid enough to express.

But she did wonder where Meggie's husband was. No one had commented on his absence. Meggie seemed in high spirits, however, laughing, joking, cutting up with all the men who looked at her with covetous expressions. At one point Meggie herded Kay and the four bachelors in front of the fireplace for a group photo. And Kay loved it when Quinn leaned over to kiss her cheek just as the flash went off.

Glancing up from where she was sitting next to

Linda Scofield at the kitchen table, she caught Quinn watching her with those gray eyes the same brooding color as the snow-heavy clouds that hovered over the town. He winked and Kay felt a now familiar thrill.

Where have you been all my life, wilderness man? The question floated unbidden into her head, lodged there and refused to leave.

She had to be careful. As wonderful as Quinn was, she couldn't allow her feelings for him to become anything more than physical. This infatuation brewing inside her was just that, infatuation. She was intrigued by their differences, turned on by his complete opposition to all the other men she had ever known.

Plus, she liked the way she changed whenever she was around him. Already, in less than a week's time, she'd began to relax, to let her hair down, to explore the part of her psyche she'd kept shut away for so many years and to abolish her old thought processes.

Kay was also impressed with Quinn's family and friends. They were close-knit and yet very welcoming to a stranger from New York City. Yes, she had to be very careful not to mistake this infatuation for something more. The last thing she wanted was to hurt him.

Or herself.

Quinn moved across the room toward her as if called by the glance she'd sent him. He lowered his head and placed a hand on her shoulder. At the pressure of his touch, at the tickling of his warm breath in her ear, Kay's heart revved.

"Are you doing all right?" he asked.

She nodded. His chin lightly grazed her cheek and caused an immediate reaction deep in her center.

"We're a rambunctious bunch," he said. "But don't let them overwhelm you."

She shook her head to let him know she was fine.

"Bet you're not used to this kind of shindig."

"It's different," she admitted, "but a lot of fun."

"Would you like to dance?" he asked.

"To this music?"

"We can fix that."

"Where would we dance?"

"Just watch." He winked again, and Kay was warmed clean through her toes.

Quinn straightened, clapped his hands and raised his voice. "People, we're in need of a dance floor and some dance music."

Kay stared in stunned amazement as soup bowls and beer mugs were deposited on the counter and half a dozen burly men relocated the poker players to the kitchen. They scooted furniture against the wall and rolled the heavy braided living room rug back from the glossy hardwood floors as if they'd done this many times before.

Linda took a seat at the upright piano parked in the corner, and solemn Caleb Greenleaf surprised Kay by retrieving a fiddle from his truck. He perched on a wooden stool pulled up next to the piano and soon the sounds of "Cotton-eyed Joe" filled the house.

"Shall we?" Quinn held out his hand to Kay. Several other couples were already gathering on the makeshift dance floor and forming a circle.

She'd danced at many a cotillion. She'd waltzed with politicians and bankers and stockbrokers. She'd worn five-thousand-dollar dresses and sipped five-hundred-dollar champagne from crystal flutes.

But she'd never danced the two-step in front of a roaring fire on a cold winter night in someone's living room wearing blue jeans and boots and a turtleneck sweater. She'd never drunk beer from a keg or eaten sourdough bread sopped in beef stew.

And she'd never had so much fun.

All these years she'd been unfairly deprived!

From "Cotton-eyed Joe," Linda and Caleb segued into "Achy Breaky Heart" with an ease that told Kay they'd been doing this for a long time. And all the men seemed to be vying for the honor of squiring Meggie around the dance floor.

Kay didn't know the steps, so she had to follow Quinn's every move. For a large man he was amazingly graceful, stepping lightly without any of the awkwardness brawny men often possessed.

"Achy Breaky" melded into "Tennessee Waltz." Quinn took her into his arms, held her close and twirled her about the living room. She was so intent on staring up into his compelling eyes that she didn't even notice for several minutes that they were the only ones dancing.

She vaguely registered that the telephone rang and someone hollered at Meggie that it was for her. Her mind was in a dream where she noticed nothing except Quinn.

Resting her head against his broad chest, Kay inhaled his piney scent, listened to the beating of his strong heart. His hands tightened on hers and he squeezed lightly, letting her know she was safe with him.

Then, for absolutely no reason at all, a lump rose in her throat, forcing her to swallow hard to keep from crying. She was happy. Why this urge to bawl?

From childhood she'd been trained to control her emotions, to repress her feelings, deny her impulses. She'd been taught that appearances were paramount, and you conducted yourself based on what others thought of you.

Growing up rich and privileged was like living on a island with other people exactly like you. The lifestyle imposed on children of the wealthy and powerful entailed certain duties and conditions foreign to the majority of the population. There was no blending into an anonymous background. You were required to watch your step at every moment. No one trod easily on the emotions of others where money and manners mingled. This behavior resulted in an inbreeding of the spirit, too much held in, regret and silent brooding.

And Kay wanted out.

She'd wasted so much time living on her island and pretending to agree with people whose values and beliefs differed so greatly from her own. She'd expended too much effort struggling against her natural tendencies. The truth of the matter was, she'd never felt more at home than she did right now in Quinn's arms.

Tilting her head, she looked into his face. He smiled at her with a lustfulness that made her hot and achy. Then without warning, he dipped his head and kissed her, all the while moving them around the living room.

It wasn't a long kiss. Nor the most passionate he'd ever given her, but it was blindingly tender.

They danced past a clump of men gathered in one corner.

"Will you get a load of that?" old Gus whispered none too softly. "Looks like Quinn's found himself a city girl to play with until the real thing comes along."

The words, when they sunk in, stung. She wasn't considered wife material. No matter how kind, how welcoming these people seemed, she wasn't one of them and never would be.

Oh, Lord, what was she thinking? She didn't belong here. She was a New Yorker, a socialite, a magazine reporter romanticizing her first trip to Alaska.

This was why her mother warned her against public displays of affection. For the first time in her life, she'd dared to let her hair down, and look what happened. She pulled away from Quinn, but he held fast to her hand and refused to let her go. She didn't want to jerk back and make things worse.

"I need some air," she murmured, avoiding his eyes. "It's too warm in here."

"I'll get your coat," he said. "We'll take a walk to the barn."

She shook her head. "I'd rather be alone."

"No, ma'am. I can't let you go by yourself."

"Why not?" she snapped.

"Wolves out there."

"Look, I live among two-legged wolves. I think I can handle myself with the furry variety."

Linda and Caleb had stopped playing. Everyone was eyeing them. Kay clamped her jaws and headed for the kitchen. She retrieved her coat from the totem pole and rushed outside.

She didn't know why she was upset. She only knew she needed distance from Quinn so she could sort out her feelings.

It was cold outside. Very cold. Kay shivered despite the warmth of her heavy coat, woolen gloves and cap. The light from the barn some fifty yards away welcomed her. She hurried toward it and tumbled inside.

To find Meggie Drummond sitting on a bale of hay struggling to light a cigarette with an obviously shaky hand. The minute Meggie saw Kay she flung the unlit cigarette across the barn.

"Oh!" Meggie and Kay cried in unison, and then laughed.

"I'm sorry," Kay mumbled. "I didn't mean to violate your privacy."

"You didn't," Meggie admitted. "You saved me."

Kay arched an eyebrow. "How so?"

"I kicked the ciggy habit years ago, but when I get nervous, that old urge returns. I sneaked out to take a couple of drags off a cigarette Gus gave me. I'm glad you stopped me. I'd hate to harness that old monkey to my back again." Meggie grinned.

"Then I'm glad I interrupted you." Kay smiled back.

"Have a seat." Meggie scooted over and patted the hay bale.

Kay sat beside her. "What drove you to sneak off for a cigarette?" her inquisitive reporter instincts made her ask.

"Mom's ankle. Looks like she's going to have to have surgery. It's not healing the way they hoped." Meggie gave her a convenient excuse, but Kay had a feeling something else was on her new friend's mind. Should she pry?

"I'm sorry to hear that."

"Yeah." Meggie made a face. "Means Mom will need me to stay through the summer, and I hate being away from home that long."

Kay nodded. "Your job?"

"Yeah, the job." Meggie shrugged nonchalantly. But Kay could tell from the expression on her face that there was something else on Meggie's mind.

Suddenly Meggie brightened. "Looks like you and Quinn are really hitting it off."

"We like each other."

"He's a great guy, and I really like you, Kay. But as one city girl to another, I have to warn you about something if you think you might be getting serious about my brother."

"Oh, don't worry. We're not serious. I know Quinn's looking for a wife, and I'm a New Yorker through and through. Couldn't live anywhere else," Kay denied, and waved a hand.

"That's good." Meggie nodded. "Because you can take an Alaskan man out of Alaska, but you can't take Alaska out of the man."

"Is that how it is with your husband, Jesse?" Kay asked, struggling to tamp down the odd strangeness pressing against her heart. Meggie's words were not a new revelation, but what she'd said underscored what Kay knew. The gulf between Quinn and her was simply too wide to breach.

"Jesse?" Meggie's eyes darkened with an emotion Kay couldn't pinpoint. An emotion akin to pain. Was her marriage in trouble? "Oh, no, Jesse's not a native Alaskan. He moved here as a teenager when his father married Caleb's mother. Jesse is pure big city. Which I suppose is what attracted me to him. I wanted so much to get out of Bear Creek, and Jesse was always talking about the places where he was going to go and the things he was going to do. He really turned my seventeen-year-old head."

"And everything worked out for you. You got what you wanted."

"Yeah," Meggie said, but it sounded as if she was still trying to convince herself of that fact. She rose to her feet. "I better get back inside. Been nice dishing the dirt with you, girlfriend."

Kay wiggled her fingers, watched Meggie walk

away and realized then they had something else in common besides their love of cities. Neither of them liked to trot their feelings out for others to examine, and deep down inside, they were both very lonely.

QUINN GLANCED about the room and waved a hand. "Everyone go on dancing."

"Can't, the two beautiful single ladies are gone," someone said.

"You're out of your league with that New Yorker, boy," old Gus cackled. "She's too high-class for you. Best to stick with your own kind."

Jake came over and clapped Quinn on the back. "Don't pay attention to Gus. You know how he likes to stir up trouble."

Irritated, Quinn stalked to the kitchen and paced. He wanted to give Kay some space, but he felt antsy. After five minutes of waiting for her to return, he couldn't stand it anymore and went out to find her.

The darkness was thick. The overcast sky obscured any chance of seeing the aurora tonight. A muted light from the barn was the only illumination.

Winding his way past the vehicles parked in an uneven grid across the driveway, he cupped his hands around his mouth and called, "Kay."

Silence.

What was the matter? he fretted. What had he done wrong?

"Kay," he called again.

Still no reply.

He was aware of a strange pounding in his chest, a burgeoning fear he couldn't seem to control. What if something had happened to her? What if she'd stepped into a hole and twisted her ankle, or worse?

His treacherous mind conjured up a hundred different horrific scenarios that had almost a zero percent chance of actually happening. But when it came to winter in Alaska, all bets were off, and Kay was a babe in the woods.

Of course, she probably went into the barn to get out of the wind, he told himself. He increased his stride, reached the barn door in a few paces and flung it open. Startled horses and cows raised their heads from their stalls to gaze at him.

He sprinted across the cement floor, examining each nook and cranny. No Kay.

By the time he burst outside again, his chest heaving, his body drenched in sweat, real fear had latched hold of his gut and wouldn't let go.

"Kay!" he shouted, panic rising.

"I'm right here, Quinn," she replied in a tone as untroubled as a frozen lake.

He skidded to a halt and jerked his head in the direction of her voice.

She was sitting in his truck, and she'd rolled the window down to speak to him. He trotted over.

"There you are." He smiled, goofy with relief.

He rounded the hood of the truck. She rolled up the passenger-side window. He climbed in beside her and started the engine. It responded sluggishly at first, then took hold. He switched on the heater, then turned in his seat to look at her.

"What happened back there?"

She shook her head. "Nothing."

"Liar." He reached out, ensnared one of her gloved hands in his. "We were having a good time, then you changed just like that." He snapped his fingers.

"Really, Quinn, you're making a much bigger deal

of this than it is.'' Her breath fogged the darkness between them.

''Did I do something to offend you?''

''It wasn't you.'' She stared out the windshield.

''What, then?''

She shrugged and in that slight gesture, he felt her pain. She was hurting and he didn't know why.

''Talk to me. Please.''

''I overheard someone make a valid observation. I guess that's why it hit a little too close to home.''

''What did they say?'' Quinn asked a second time through clenched teeth.

Kay stared down at their entwined hands. ''You heard old Gus. He said I was nothing to you but a playmate until the real thing came along.''

Quinn's breath caught. ''And you believe that?''

''Yes. You are looking for a wife, and I'm certainly not what you had in mind when you concocted that ad.''

''Look at me,'' he commanded.

She raised her chin, met his eyes with a steadfast gaze. She was so good at cloaking her feelings when she wanted to. She was putting up barriers, keeping him from getting too close.

''Would you like to be more than just my sexual playmate?'' Quinn asked, barely daring to hope that she might say yes.

Kay laughed. ''Of course not. We're at opposite places in our lives. You're ready for marriage, and I just got out of a lousy relationship. I've got a lot to learn about myself before I can be with any man.''

His hopes sank as quickly as they'd buoyed. So much for wishing on a star.

''That man's comment,'' she continued, ''simply

brought home to me how different we really are. How much a fish out of water I am here."

He squeezed her hand. "Sweetheart, don't let what other people think bother you so much."

"That's hard for me. I was raised to believe the opinion of others matters a great deal."

"You're going to have to get over this need to please everyone." He traced a finger along her jawline. "Or you'll never please yourself."

"I know."

"We'll have to address this issue in our next love lesson. Obviously it's deep-seated. In fact, I think we may have stumbled onto the real reason you've never been able to have an orgasm. You are repressed."

"Tell me, Doctor—" she laughed again "—is there any hope for me?"

"As long as you have that sense of humor, there's always hope."

In that moment she looked so forlorn he knew that the laughter was merely a cover. She really feared that she could never have an orgasm.

He shook his head in disbelief, wondering where she'd gotten such an idea. Frigid women didn't wear stockings and garters and sexy black lace bras. They didn't travel more than three thousand miles in search of sexual release. He admired her courage more than he could say, and he was even more determined than ever to help this amazing woman achieve her goal.

Quinn hauled her across the seat toward him, wrapped his arms around her. Her pale hair shone in the darkness, her tantalizing feminine scent filling his nostrils. He was overwhelmed with myriad sensations, and he didn't fully understand a single one of them. Except for a flourishing need that was both distinguishable and unequaled. Lust. Yet wildly stronger than lust.

His body ached to be joined with hers. He wanted to be buried inside her. He longed to hear her soft cries of encouragement, yearned to feel the satisfying clench of her love muscles around his erection as he thrust deeper and deeper until she began to be a part of him.

Kay was as eager as he. Her lips parted in anticipation; her breathing sped up.

"And you want me?" she whispered.

He guided her hand to his rock-solid erection. "You tell me."

She gasped, and in the glow from the dashboard, he saw her eyes widen. "You're so hard."

"That's what you do to me, Kay."

He kissed her then, inhaled her sweet, sweet taste and reveled in the heat of her mouth against his. Every time he kissed her, it felt like the first time. He marveled at everything about her. Her flavor, her scent, the plushness of her pampered skin. He felt as if he was tumbling down a long, dark hole, and he didn't care one whit that it was bottomless.

She made muted noises of pleasure, and he almost came right then and there. He pulled away, panting slightly.

The rasp of their breathing filled the cab of the truck.

"What's wrong?" she asked.

"Nothing's wrong. I want you more than I've ever wanted any woman. I want you so much it literally causes me pain."

She trembled against his chest. "Oh, Quinn, I want you that way, too. I never knew my body's hunger could be so overpowering."

"Neither did I, sweetheart, neither did I."

Then without warning she scooted her tush across the seat until her hot body was flush with his. She pressed those sweet, honeyed lips to the pulse at his throat and lightly bit down. She ran a hand up the nape of his neck, entangled her fingers in his hair and stoked little swirl patterns that sent spikes of hard desire shoving through him.

"What are you doing?" His voice was so husky, so soaked with desire, he could scarcely hear the words.

"Take me home with you," she whispered between nibbles. "Take me home and make love to me right now."

"You have no idea how much I'd like to do exactly that."

"So put the truck in gear and let's get out of here."

He shook his head. "We can't."

"Why not?" Her lips puckered into a pout.

"Because," he said, "you're still not ready."

11

WHAT DID HE MEAN she wasn't ready? If he didn't make love to her soon, Kay was going to split in two.

He'd left her on the front porch of the B&B last night with the promise he'd pick her up the following evening to continue her love lessons. But that wasn't enough. She wanted more and she wanted it now.

Kay stared at the screen of her laptop computer, at what she'd written more than four hours earlier and hadn't added a word to since: "During early March in Bear Creek, needle-cold wind rinses every impurity from the air."

But that sharp cold did nothing to dispel her impure thoughts. In fact, the weather seemed to escalate her horniness. Face it, her brain was mush. Courtesy of Quinn Scofield.

The tease.

She was beginning to think he was enjoying torturing her far too much. What was he planning now?

The knock at her bedroom door startled her. She slid off the bed and padded over to throw it open. And was brightened to see Quinn standing there with a large, brown paper bag in his hand.

She glanced at her watch, then back at him. "You're way early."

"I know. Thought I'd catch you off guard."

"I'm not ready." She gestured at her long-sleeved T-shirt layered over powder-blue long johns.

"We're not going anywhere."

"We're not?"

"Nope. I decided to bring the party to you."

"Oh?" Warily she eyed the bag. "What's in there?"

"Curiosity killed the cat."

"Satisfaction brought him back."

"Precisely." He shouldered past her and his big frame seemed to fill the whole room. Kay kicked the door closed behind him.

"Ah." He set the bag down on her dressing table and nodded at her laptop. "You're working on the article. Am I interrupting?"

"Not at all. I was done for the day." She skipped over to the computer and slammed the top down. She didn't want him seeing what pitiful little she'd written and figuring out he was responsible for her writer's block.

"Don't you think you should save your work before you lose it?" he asked.

One sentence. How tough would it be to lose one sentence?

"I already saved." She circled closer to the paper bag, hoping to get a peek inside.

But Quinn was quicker. He clamped a hand around the top. "Ah-ah, no peeking."

"You're driving me right out of my skull. I hope you know that." Then she did something completely out of character for a self-possessed, controlled Freemont. She stuck her tongue out at him.

It felt great. It felt freeing. And it made Quinn laugh.

She liked making him laugh.

"Yeah," he said. "You better be careful the way you use that thing. I can think of several good uses for a sexy tongue."

"You're all talk, big boy," she challenged, squaring off with him toe-to-toe. "You had your chance last night and you blew it."

"That's why I'm here. To make amends."

"Yes?" She perked up at the offer. Was he actually going to make love to her this time?

"The real reason I came over here, instead of taking you to my place, is that Jake's rooms all come complete with those nice, deep, oversize whirlpool-jet bathtubs."

"Meaning?"

Oh, she was enjoying herself.

Quinn reached for the sack and with excruciatingly slow movements removed first a bottle of foaming bath oil and then a package of floating candles.

Kay grinned. Was this guy romantic or what?

"I'll run the bath," he said. "You slip into your robe and pin up your hair."

He went into the adjoining bathroom. Kay heard the water come on and she couldn't get naked fast enough. She stripped off her T-shirt and long johns and wrapped a fluffy white bathrobe around her body. She peeled off her socks, nudged her feet into house slippers, then twisted her hair up off her neck and pinned it in place with a couple of bobby pins.

By the time she edged into the bathroom to join Quinn, the mirrors were already steamed over.

Watching her walk into the room made Quinn's pulse jump. One sleeve of her too-large bathrobe had slipped down on her shoulder, exposing a slender collarbone and an enticing expanse of creamy-white skin.

He almost dropped the bath oil and felt himself grow instantly hard with desire for her.

God, she was gorgeous.

She crossed the room toward him. Quinn gulped and backed up as far as he could, until a towel rack poked him in the shoulder blades. Holy cow, what was she doing?

She went up on tiptoe, cocked her head and lightly brushed her lips over his before lowering her heels to the floor again.

Yo, Mama!

She nuzzled his neck, her labored breathing fanning warmly across his flesh. He tried not to think about their perfect fit, his throbbing arousal and how easy it would be to surrender to temptation and take her right here on the bathroom floor. She was extracting her revenge, torturing him the way he'd been torturing her for days. And he was defenseless against her.

He kissed her ear, then ran a tongue along the faint scar traversing her skin from her ear to her jaw. "How'd you get the scar?"

She shivered into his chest. "Who cares?"

"I do," he whispered. "I want to know everything about you."

"Why?" She raised her head so she could study his face.

"You're interesting." He traced a finger along the scar.

She made a dismissive noise.

"You're not going to tell me?"

Dropping her gaze, she shrugged. "Not much to tell. It happened during the one and only time my mother let me play with the maid's children. For weeks I'd begged to be allowed to join in their fun. We were running and diving on a Slip-and-Slide when I slipped off the slide and slammed into a yard ornament.'' She raised a hand to the scar. ''I had to have six stitches.''

''Your mother never let you play with those kids again?''

''That was the end of my Slip-and-Slide days. Mummy said the maid's children were ruffians. That they'd maimed me for life.''

''I love your scar,'' he declared fiercely.

''My mother still hounds me about getting plastic surgery. But it's such a small mark, and to tell the truth, I was always a little proud of my battle wound.'' She smiled.

''I hate to say this sweetheart, but your mother...'' He shook his head, let his words trail off. He didn't want to bad-mouth her mother, but the more he found out about Kay's family, the more he understood why she was so emotionally repressed.

''Shh,'' she said. ''No more talking.''

Lifting her shoulders, she untied her sash and the next thing he knew, the bathrobe lay in a circle about her feet.

He swallowed. Hard. And waved at the tub.

Kay pushed a tendril of loose hair from her face and met his gaze. There was no mistaking the appreciation in his eyes as he visually caressed her body. That and the slight groan that slipped from his lips let her know how much he wanted her.

Suddenly she felt self-conscious. *Freemont women don't get naked and splash around in the bath with men they barely know.*

That thought overrode her hesitancy. She wanted to do the exact opposite of what a Freemont woman would do. Face it, Freemont women were fuddy-duds who tolerated adulterous husbands and sublimated their sexuality through shopping sprees and plastic surgery. Did she want to end up like her mother and her grandmother and her aunts and female cousins? All superficial women with nothing more to concern themselves with than the latest fall fashions or which bedroom to redecorate next or how many people to invite to their summer soirée. None of them had real marriages or real jobs or expressed authentic feelings.

She raised her head again, determined to see this through, and noticed Quinn was wincing. Her gaze trailed lower, and she spotted the source of his discomfort—the erection pushing against his zipper.

He was watching her, his eyes taking in every curve and dip of her body. His glance traveled from her shoulders to her breasts to her waist and lower. Up and down the length of her legs, then stopped to linger a moment at the blond triangle between her thighs.

Awareness and a dazzling heat prickled her skin. She'd never felt so exposed. She'd thought that night in the sauna had been sexually charged, but then, because of a silk blindfold, she'd been unable to read his reaction to her body. Now she saw every erotic thought that crossed his face. And the power she held over him blew her away.

Her entire body flushed with the heat of his stare. Damn. She'd never blushed so much in her life as she had around him. That unabashed stare of his caused her heart to do the conga against her rib cage. Her hormones were flipping like acrobats in the far recesses of her groin.

He made her feel special, and yet she had no right to feel that way. Quinn was a ladies' man. No doubt about it. From that wolfish grin to the romantic bath complete with bubbles and candles, it was clear he appreciated women. Right now he was appreciating her for all he was worth, and she was helpless against his charms.

It wasn't that men hadn't told her she was beautiful before. She'd had many admirers. The trouble was, because of her own lack of sexual interest in them, she hadn't believed their flattery. She figured that, like Lloyd, they were interested only in her wealth, her family's reputation, her blueblood pedigree.

But Quinn was different. He made her feel a thousand times a woman, and he didn't seem to care one whit that she came from blue-blood stock or that her family oozed money.

Funny that the man she was most attracted to would be the man she couldn't have in the long term.

Ha, ha, good one, Fate. The joke's on me.

Because despite her best intentions not to get emotionally involved with Quinn, he had a sneaky way of flying under her radar, weakening her defenses, slashing right to the root of her intimate longings. It was if he knew what was in her heart and in her mind.

Spooky stuff.

Enough to make her rethink this whole orgasm business.

When had things gotten so complicated?

Just go along for the ride, she told herself. Savor every step of the way with this star-kissed man. Abandon all caution. Bestow yourself on him here and now. Accept what he can offer you; don't pine for more.

This extraordinary man was giving new life to her parched body, waking up her sleeping soul. For that, she would be eternally grateful.

He tipped his head in that rakish way he had, and a

lock of whiskey-colored hair fell across his brow. He arched an eyebrow expectantly. ''Well? Are you going to get in the bath or not?''

Well, indeed.

Here goes nothing.

Gingerly she stepped into the bubbling water, then sank into the steamy depths. A moan of pleasure escaped her lips as her muscles at first flexed and then relaxed, soothed by the pulsating jets and silky heat of the water. It felt as if she was sliding into a tub of liquefied butter. Hot, thick and sinfully delicious.

''Good girl,'' he murmured, and knelt beside the tub. ''The point here is to get you completely relaxed.''

''I'm well on the way.''

''Close your eyes.''

The corners of her mouth tipped up in a smile, and she let her eyelids drift closed. In a moment she felt Quinn's hand on her fingers, oh-so-leisurely massaging each knuckle.

She didn't know what to expect. Anything and everything he did was a wondrous surprise. From her hand, he advanced to her wrist, then ran his fingers, in a feather-soft stroke, up and down the delicate underside of her forearms.

Kay shivered, alarmed at the intensity of the sensation. ''No, don't, it's too much.''

''Shh,'' he soothed, and kept stroking. In a moment the tickling sensation passed and she began to enjoy herself.

He massaged each arm, then turned his attention to her feet.

''Oooh.'' She sighed as his fingers kneaded her toes, the balls of her feet, her heels.

His tender massage seemed to last forever. When she thought she might fall asleep she was so relaxed, he moved up her legs to her calves and there, he applied hard pressure that made her groan. When his fingers brushed the erogenous area behind her knees, she almost came undone.

She waited for his hand to slide upward to her thighs and beyond, but he disappointed her and stopped. She opened one eye, saw him soaping up a sponge with vanilla-scented bath soap. She smelled the homey, sweet aroma as it clung to drops of steamy air.

He rubbed her shoulders with the sponge, then ran it over her breasts. Kay sucked in a breath. Her nipples beaded and begged for more attention. He washed her belly, then her thighs, but he completely avoided the part of her she most wanted him to touch.

He was doing this on purpose, she thought, working her to a fever-pitch, then dropping her like a skydiver without a parachute.

She shifted position and spread her legs, hoping to tempt him to go farther, explore more. Water sloshed over the edge of the tub, soaking his shirt. She looked up at him and smirked. She could see his nipples had beaded as tight and hard as her own.

''Whoa there,'' he said, his voice husky. ''Slow down, sweetheart, we've got hours and hours yet to go.''

She heard a whimpering noise then and realized the sound came from her. ''I can't stand much more of this, Quinn.''

''Oh, baby, we're just getting started.'' He pampered her like a mother coddling her small child. He turned off the jets, lit the scented candles and set them in the water to float beside her. The heady aroma of a spring floral bouquet curled through her nose. Jasmine, lavender, honeysuckle.

He got up, turned out the lights, then sat back down beside her and took her hands. "Now stare at the candles, inhale deeply and concentrate on your body for a few minutes."

She blinked at him.

"Go ahead, do it."

She closed her eyes again, leaned her head back against the tub and inhaled deeply. She'd tried meditation, of course. And creative visualization and yoga classes. She'd heard rave reviews of all these techniques to enhance your sex life, but she'd never been able to relax. Something had always held her back. She felt odd letting herself go in the company of strangers, and she'd never been able to freely express herself like everyone else in the classes.

But here now, for the first time, she felt her body floating as if on a cloud, while at the same time she felt leaden, affixed to the tub. It was an exhilarating experience.

"That's right," he whispered as if he knew she'd achieved an exalted state. "Focus your attention on the center of your belly."

She did as he asked.

"As you breathe in, imagine a warm light settling in your solar plexus and gradually spreading outward."

How had he become so sophisticated about such things? she wanted to ask. Living out here in the wilderness, so far from people and activities.

But she couldn't ask him this, because she was supposed to be concentrating. Yet it was hard to focus when she could smell his masculine scent even over the flowery aroma of the candles.

Warm glow. That was it.

Then like a match to a wick, her belly suddenly did feel hot. Hot and tingly. She rode the sensation, imagining the heat spreading out, coursing through her body, pooling in her groin.

And then she was so hot she couldn't stand it a second more. The power she had over her own body was eerie. She'd never been so in touch with herself.

Her eyes flew open and she found Quinn watching her in the candlelight.

"Pretty awesome, huh?"

All she could do was nod.

"Okay," he said. "Time to get out, your fingers are turning pruney."

He got to his feet, opened a fluffy bath towel and held his hand out to her.

When she touched him, the contact amazed her. Quinn wrapped the towel around her dripping body. He rubbed her dry. The towel was new, mildly scratchy. Her skin was pink from the heat, the water, the brisk toweling.

His affectionate attention reminded her of the nanny she'd had as a little girl. After her bath, Nanny Marie would dust her with talcum powder, help her into her pajamas and then sit by Kay's bed reading one of her favorite books for the millionth time until she fell asleep. Once in a while, on her way to a party, Mommy would pop into her room to say good-night. But she never hugged or nuzzled her cheek the way Nanny did. Honoria wouldn't risk smearing her makeup or mussing her elaborate hairstyle by bending over to kiss her daughter.

Kay blew out her breath, pushed away the melancholy memory. This wasn't the time or place for a stumble down memory lane.

"You okay?" Quinn asked, his gaze on her face.

"Fine." She forced a smile.

Once she was dry, he took her hand and guided her into the bedroom. "Lie down on the bed on your stomach."

"I feel guilty," she said. "You're doing all these things for me, and I've done nothing for you."

"Hush. My time will come. Tonight is all about you."

She lay then, on her belly, with her face pressed into the pillow. Outside she could hear winter spitting icy rain against the windowpane, but inside they were wrapped tight in a snug cocoon.

Quinn sat on the edge of the bed beside her. The mattress sagged under his weight. His hand, warm and slick with heated peach-scented oil, slid over the planes of her back, lightly caressing.

Had anything in the world ever felt this luxurious?

His hands advanced in ever-widening circles, down her spine to her lower back and then to her buttocks, which he teased with firmer caresses.

She felt sexy deep in the most intimate part of her. Sexy and wet and desperate for this man. She tried to turn over, to face him, to see what he was thinking, but he pushed softly on her shoulder.

"Not yet."

She groaned. "Bastard."

"Now, now. No call for such language." He laughed. "You'll be thanking me soon enough."

"Pretty damn sure of yourself, aren't you?" she said through gritted teeth.

"Don't you know it."

His motions changed but never stopped. Short strokes to long strokes and back again, he swept his hand up and down her back until she felt as if she'd melted into the sheets.

"Turn over," he said.

She barely had the energy, but she managed.

His big hands slid down her neck. Mentally, her mind went where his fingers were. Butterfly pressure on her throat. Tingles in the hollow spot where her collarbones met.

Hot, cold. Soft, hard. She felt so many things.

Her breath caught in her lungs when his right hand made a leisurely foray from her hip to her left breast, kneading with gentle, rhythmic motion that had her squirming even more.

His hand grazed her hardened nipple, and she sank her teeth into her bottom lip to keep from crying out. He leaned in close, ran his tongue over that insatiable nipple, tugging, licking, suckling until her breathing was nothing but shallow, ragged gasps.

His splayed palm felt different than his fist. He used both to fondle her. First one, then the other. Round and square, up and down. Opened, closed. Curved, straight.

After what seemed an eternity, his fingers finally skated to her belly button.

She writhed as his hand lingered there. "Don't," she said breathlessly. "I'm ticklish."

"That means you've got a lot of sexual energy stored there. We need to release it. Let it flow throughout your entire system."

Then he leaned over and pressed his lips to her navel. His hair glinted in the light from the bedside lamp.

No one had ever kissed her belly button before, and she found it wildly erotic.

But then the next thing she knew, he'd left there and was headed decidedly south.

What was this?

With one hand he gently spread her knees. "Hold still," he commanded. "Keep your eyes shut."

She closed her eyes, felt his weight shift off the bed. In a minute he was back. She heard what sounded like jar lids being opened. She cracked one eye to see what in the heck he was doing.

"No peeking."

"What's going on?"

"Lie back and enjoy the ride."

She tried to sink into the pillow, to let her body go limp, but she was so damned curious. "I can't stand this. Tell me what you're doing."

"Pretending I'm Michelangelo. I've always wanted to paint a masterpiece."

"What?" She frowned.

"Shh," he whispered, and she felt a soft feathering of a dry artist's paintbrush sweep against her furrowed brow.

Everywhere the brush touched, she burst into flames. Down he went, traversing her body for a second time.

Eyebrows, eyelids, cheeks, nose, lips. He worked his way around first one ear and then the other, then slipped to the underside of her jaw.

He took the brush away, and when he brought it back, it was warm and wet.

"What's that?" she asked.

"Open your mouth."

She parted her lips. He leaned over and lightly dabbed something on the tip of her tongue.

"Mmm. Chocolate body paint."

"Very good."

With bold strokes, he painted a wide stripe straight down between her breasts to her tummy. Her toes curled at the delicious sensation. He drew a design around her belly button.

"What's that?" he asked.

"A heart." She grinned.

"And this?"

She felt him spell out K-A-Y. "My name."

He switched to a tiny brush and swirled it around her nipples. "Yes," he hissed triumphantly. "I love how they glisten when they stand perkily at attention."

Was she still on planet Earth? Or had she been shot clean into outer space?

He returned to her knees, edged them apart again. "There we go. I'm switching to my smallest tool."

"Wh...?" she started to ask but got no further.

His sizzling-hot hands rested at the apex of her thighs. And he was manipulating that brush like Michelangelo himself. The tip was wet and hot and sticky and oh-so-fine. And he definitely knew how to use it. He gently eased back the flesh protecting her womanhood and caressed the hard, thrusting nub with the warm, damp sable of the brush.

The sensation was nothing short of electric.

She inhaled all the way to her feet. She felt every velvety strand of the brush's thick fur as it fluttered back and forth over her flowering cleft. She swung her hips, gyrating against the brush, reveling in his sounds of approval.

"Yes, baby, yes," he purred.

He flicked the brush. Back and forth, back and forth until she was covered in steamy chocolate.

"Now," he said, "I'm going to lick you clean."

He dipped his head. His hair rasped against her belly. He was licking at the high recesses of the inside of her thigh. So near the area where she was dying for him to be. She was tired of this torment. She wanted to feel his hard, throbbing member thrusting deep inside her.

She smelled his maleness, and his scent spurred her arousal. Her body, which minutes before had been soft and pliant from the bath and the sensual rub, was now stiff and ready. She was wet, so incredibly wet. She wanted it. This spectacular release everyone spoke of. This colorful, vibrant fantastic orgasm. It was possible. Within her reach at last. She could feel it building, feel herself getting more strung out and desperate.

She tossed her head like a restless mare. She arched against his mouth, wanting, no, needing more, more. Her nerves were raw, ragged.

His tongue, oh, sweet heaven, his tongue! She unfurled to him like a rosebud opening to the sun, exalting in the heat, blooming, growing, expanding.

He was too slow. He was taking too long. This was maddening. This was incredible. This was hell. This was heaven.

Was it possible to feel so much driving need and not collapse if that need was not met?

"Take me, Quinn," she begged, unable to stand this one second longer. "Make love with me. Get inside me. I want you."

But he diligently ignored her pleas, still slowly, gently licking her with his tongue.

He inched closer and closer to the prize, his mouth

now between her thighs and her outer lips. He drew circles with his tongue and each lick felt like a stinging-hot brand. Whimpering, she pushed her hips upward, her lower back clearing the bed.

And then he was flicking his tongue across her aching cleft while at the same time stroking the sensitive area just below with his fingers. She cried out at the dual sensation. She was falling, stumbling, careening into a caldron of heat.

Boiling, baking, blistering heat.

Hijacked, bushwhacked, shanghaied.

He'd kidnapped her, mind, body and soul.

She tried to say something, but her tongue wouldn't work. Her ears rang.

I need, I need, I need.

So this was what it was all about. This was why everyone extolled sex as if it was some great curative. She felt as if she was hanging on the edge of a precipice by her fingernails.

She was aflame, ablaze, incandescent. She was the aurora borealis, and Quinn's dangerous, exquisite mouth created sunspots, shooting highly charged energy through her until she was aglow with electricity.

She gyrated and rotated. She writhed and bucked.

Make it happen, she begged silently, hungering to tumble over into that magical abyss.

His tongue loved her, caressed her, lifted her to the pinnacle.

She waited for the drop, entwined her fingers in his hair and waited with bated breath, knew that orgasm was only seconds away. At last. After twenty-seven years. At last.

And then, just before she came, he stopped.

12

"NO," SHE WHIMPERED. "No. You can't stop now."

Quinn looked down into her face, scrunched tight with both pain and pleasure, and his gut torqued. How he wanted her! If only she knew how difficult this was for him, holding back when more than anything in the world he ached to bury himself deep inside her and stay there forever.

She raised herself on her elbows, flicked out her tongue and licked his throat. "Please," she whispered, her eyes still effulgent with the sheen of lust. "Please."

He almost lost his minuscule shard of control and took her, but his overwhelming desire to confer upon her the precious gift of her first orgasm kept him tethered to his goal.

"One more night, sweetheart." He pressed his mouth to her ear. "Just one more night. Trust me on this."

Kay groaned and sank against him. "Quinn, this is cruel and unusual punishment."

"I know, baby, I know." He gently caressed her head. "But it's for your own good. Tomorrow night, my place. I promise."

But could he keep that promise? She'd been close to orgasm just now, but if he'd continued stroking her, would she have plunged over the edge or remained on the precipice, unable to make the plunge? Was that the real reason he'd pulled the plug on tonight's proceedings? Because he was afraid that, when push came to shove, he couldn't deliver on his promise?

The thought of letting her down, of not being able to fulfill her sexually, caused a clutch of anxiety in the bottom of his heart. God, how he wanted to be the one to make her happy.

That was why he wouldn't give in to those pleading eyes and his raging hormones. That was why they had to wait one more night. Everything had to be perfect. Tomorrow night he was pulling out all the stops, unpacking his arsenal, opening his bag of tricks. He was going to make sure she had the sexual experience of a lifetime and return home to New York with treasured memories of Alaska that would never fade.

For some odd reason he felt empty at the thought of her leaving. He'd known from the beginning that this could not be a long-term relationship, that for many reasons they weren't well suited as a couple, but he'd hardly had any time to get to know her the way he wanted to know her.

"Quinn?" She reached up and traced his lips with a finger. "Is something wrong?"

Wrong? Oh, only that he was holding an exquisite angel in his arms and soon he would have to let her go. He feared that consummating their passion, joining their bodies and taking their relationship to the highest physical level would make things that much harder.

And yet, he could not, would not, let her down, even if it meant getting hurt himself. She was worth the sacrifice. He would award her all he had to give.

"Nothing." He smiled. No point tormenting himself

over something that could not be changed. "Just planning tomorrow night."

She curled against his body. "I can't wait," she whispered, "to see what you've prepared for me."

Oh, boy. The pressure was on, and somehow, he would rise to the challenge. But how could he provide Kay with what she needed while at the same time keeping himself from falling head over heels in love?

"Kiss me again," she whispered. "Just kissing and nothing else."

How could he refuse that?

Kay sighed into his mouth. This man was so powerful and yet so tender. He was controlled and yet willing to do whatever she asked of him. She'd never met anyone like him.

They lay on the bed together, side by side, his tongue softly exploring her mouth.

In her mind, a vision appeared. She saw him in her mind's eye as clearly as if it was happening. He was cuddling a sweet newborn baby in the crook of his arm, gazing tenderly into the baby's face. His hands were bigger than the baby's tiny head. The explicit contrast was startling.

He would make a wonderful father.

Kay opened her eyes, stared at Quinn, who was looking right at her. Why was she picturing him as a father? Why was she thinking about babies? When she'd been with Lloyd, she'd barely given babies a second thought. Oh, she supposed she wanted a child someday. But she'd been too consumed with her career, too unimpressed with Lloyd to spend much time fantasizing about babies. Now, in a sudden rush, all those maternal feelings she'd suppressed came to the forefront of her mind, confusing the hell out of her.

She couldn't have him. She could never be the kind of wife he needed, so why daydream about having his baby? She pulled away from him, disturbed by her feelings.

"What's wrong?" His husky words clobbered her thoughts, demanded entry into the part of her she kept most private—her heart.

She struggled for her famous Freemont control, tried to force her features into expressionless lines.

And failed miserably.

She couldn't keep dragging that tired facade over her face, couldn't keep hiding her true feelings.

Quinn reached out and gently massaged her shoulder. "Tell me, sweetheart, have I done something wrong?"

In that moment Kay lost it completely, and to her horror, she began to cry.

"What is it?" Alarmed, Quinn sat up. His heart thundered. What had he done wrong? He gathered her to his chest. "Talk to me."

"Nothing." She shook her head. "It's just that no one man has ever treated me so gently, so kindly."

He squeezed her tight. "Well, darling, your luck has just changed."

Concern for her, and another emotion he wasn't quite ready to name, filled his chest. He searched for the right words to say, to tell her how special she was, when the beeper he wore for fire-call emergencies went off.

THEY CAREENED down the street, headed for the fire. Kay's blood was pumping through her veins like Freon. Quinn had agreed to take her along as a journalist as long as she promised to stay clear of the fire.

He gripped the steering wheel in his hands, his gaze focused intently on the icy road in front of them. Through the two-way radio mounted on the dash, he was in touch with the other firefighters and had learned that Millie Peterson's house was on fire.

Millie, Quinn told her, was an eighty-five-year-old widow who lived just outside Bear Creek. She'd grown absentminded of late, and he worried that maybe she'd forgotten to turn the stove off before she went to bed. He gave the truck more gas and took the curve far too fast. Kay, thankful for her seat belt, gripped the armrest and prayed that Millie was all right.

Quinn braked to a stop outside a small, two-story frame house at the same instant that Mack, Jake, Caleb and a couple of other men arrived in the fire truck. Orange flames licked their way across the roof. The acrid smell of smoke consumed the air. Quinn sprinted over to the truck.

Kay got out and watched him quickly and methodically go about the business of putting out a fire. She wanted to help. Needed to keep busy so she wouldn't worry so much about Quinn and the other firefighters. Glancing around, Kay saw an elderly woman standing on the lawn. She hurried over.

"Millie?" she asked.

The elderly lady, dressed in long johns and a bathrobe, was shivering, her glasses askew on her wrinkled face. Kay whipped off her coat and draped it around Millie's shoulders.

"Doodles," Millie cried. "My little doggy, Doodles, is inside."

"I'll tell the firemen," Kay said, and raced over to Quinn, who was breaking out an ax from the back of the truck. ''Quinn,'' she called to him. He raised his head. ''Millie's dog is inside.''

Quinn glanced toward the house. In the short time they'd been here, the flames had grown taller, arched higher into the night sky. Mack grabbed Quinn's arm. ''Don't do it, man. The house is about to go.''

''Doodles!'' Millie wailed, and wrung her hands.

''I've got to try,'' Quinn said. ''Millie would give up and die if anything happened to that dog.''

''Quinn,'' Kay whimpered, ''be careful.''

''Don't worry, honey. I'll be back.'' He leaned down and placed a quick kiss on her lips. ''I promise.''

While Mack and Jake turned the fire hose on the house, Quinn charged through the front door.

Kay's heart crammed into her throat and stayed there.

''I'm scared,'' Millie said.

Kay surprised herself by confessing, ''Me too.'' Since coming to Bear Creek, she'd found it easier and easier to express her feelings. She didn't know if that was good or bad. She only knew that in New York she would never have felt comfortable enough to throw her arm around a frightened little old lady she didn't know and hug her close.

For what seemed an eternity, Kay and Millie huddled together, waiting. More cars arrived. A crowd gathered. At one point Kay looked around and realized the whole town was here, people running to and fro, doing what they could to help. Someone threw a blanket over her and Millie.

Kay turned to see Meggie standing behind her, a worried expression on her face. Kay nodded.

Meggie reached over, took Kay's hand and squeezed.

A huge lump of emotion formed in Kay's throat.

I'm among friends, she realized. Honest-to-gosh friends. Not just people who pretended to like her because she was rich.

Suddenly she felt a part of Alaska, a part of the community, a part of Quinn's family. But almost as suddenly, her fear quickly pushed aside her quiet feeling of acceptance. Quinn should have been out by now. Where was he?

Just as Jake said, "I'm going in after Quinn," a form appeared in the doorway of the burning house and Quinn staggered out, something clutched tightly in his arms.

Doodles.

Millie sprang forward to snatch her dog from him, and Kay sprang forward to scoop her smoky, cinder-smeared man into her arms, unmindful of the hubbub surrounding them.

Quinn picked her up. She wrapped her legs around his waist and her arms around his neck.

"You're safe," she whispered.

"I told you I'd be back," he said gruffly. "And I always keep my promises."

"I was so worried, so scared I'd never see you again."

"Were you really?"

"Of course, you big goof."

"Hey, what's this?" he asked.

Tears were streaming down her cheek and she didn't even realize it until he kissed them gently away.

TONIGHT'S THE NIGHT.

It was six o'clock on Sunday evening as Kay parked the Wagoneer that Quinn's parents had lent her, then made her way up the frozen walkway. The smell of wood smoke hung in the air. The snow crunched delightfully underfoot.

At last, at last, at last, she mentally chanted.

Underneath her coat she wore a red silk dress, sheer red-tinted stockings, a racy red garter belt and three-inch red stilettos. But in the short distance from the heated car to Quinn's front door, the icy bite of wind had turned her legs into Popsicles. Alaska in late winter was no place to wear seductive clothing.

But the sexy outfit made her feel ultrafeminine, her gift to Quinn. She hadn't considered wearing anything else.

Tonight was the night.

He opened the door and let her in.

She tilted her head at him, and the sight of his rugged profile caused a hitch in her breath. He was so handsome, so masculine, so unabashedly male. She couldn't wait to see him naked. Couldn't wait to have him inside her.

He caught her watching him and grinned. She looked away but not without holding his gaze for a long moment first. He led her inside to the rug by the fire.

"Sit," he instructed, then took her coat and went to hang it up. When he returned, he sat beside her.

An awkward silence hung between them for the briefest minute, then they both chuckled at once.

"Your feet look pale." He said. "Give 'em to me."

Languidly, as if moving through a pool of pudding, Kay raised her legs and plopped her feet in Quinn's lap. He slipped off her high heels and tossed them into the corner. The sensation of his warm fingers on her cold toes caused her to hiss in her breath.

He rubbed her feet between his palms. First the left and then the right. "I'd lecture you on dressing warmly," he said, "but you look so damned sexy in that outfit I'm not saying a word."

She laughed, pleased at his compliment. He made her feel like a seductive vamp, and she loved the feeling.

"Mmm," she moaned softly against his tender ministrations, lying back against the stone hearth and closing her eyes. "That feels wonderful."

"Are you hungry?" he asked. "Dinner's keeping warm in a Crock-Pot, so we could eat now or whenever you're ready."

"Just keep rubbing," she said, her body going eagerly limp. She amazed herself at how easily she relaxed with Quinn.

His fingers rubbed and kneaded, caressed and massaged. He moved from her feet to her ankles, then up her calf.

"How does this feel?"

"Heavenly."

"How about this?"

"Ooh, you wicked devil."

"At your service, angel."

She thrilled at his words, at the sex in his voice. Her body erupted in a shower of mind-numbing tingles.

"You have gorgeous legs," he said.

"And you administer a mean foot rub. Your hands are like a touch of silk."

"Your legs were the first thing I noticed about you. You know, on the plane to JFK."

"Really?" She opened her eyes and peered at him in the flickering glow from the firelight.

"Uh-huh. What was the first thing you noticed about me?"

"The way you kept staring at my legs."

"No kidding."

"It wasn't hard to miss. Your eyes were practically bugging out of your head."

"I didn't know you were paying any attention to me at all."

"You're a hard one to miss, Quinn Scofield."

His hands were on her knees now and climbing higher. She felt herself swept away as if drugged by a magical potion and carried off into an X-rated fantasy land.

She and Quinn are Russian nobles traveling at high speed across the snowy landscape in their troika. Their thick fur wraps protect them from the harsh Siberian winter.

Suddenly highwaymen seize them, haul them from their sled.

"Strip," the brigands demand, and in the bitter cold they peel off their garments. Now, they're going to freeze to death, together, in the bitter cold.

But highwaymen are not completely merciless, even though they are laughing at their nakedness. Before they leave, the bandits toss down a fur rug.

They wrap the skin around them and stagger toward a wooden hut at the edge of the forest. He builds a fire, and she falls asleep in his arms.

She awakes to find him rubbing the fur between her legs. Suddenly he seizes her around the waist, flips her onto her belly and he takes her from behind, while his hand stimulates her from the front. As she sinks down into the throes of climax, she hears a snowstorm howl-

ing outside the hut and knows they will not be rescued for days.

"Let me in on your fantasy," Quinn whispered. "Tell me what you're thinking."

Kay's eyes flew open and she blinked up at him. She realized his hand was on her upper thigh and so very close to the most dangerous part of her. "I don't know what you mean."

"Don't lie to me, Kay, you're no good at it." He reached out a finger and lightly stroked her cheek. "You're having an awesome sexual fantasy."

"How do you know?" Her lip quivered. She was amazed at his powers of deduction. He seemed to know her most intimate thoughts.

"You've been holding your sexuality at bay for so long you're bound to be brimming with fantasies. Tell me and we'll reenact them."

She hesitated. She'd never revealed her wildest sexual fantasies to anyone.

Was she brave enough to do this?

"Trust me," he murmured. "Share. Let me go there with you."

"Snowbound," she murmured after a long moment. She was giving him the highest degree of trust she was capable of bestowing. "In the frozen Russian tundra. We're rich nobles who've been stripped of all our wealthy trappings by bandits and left to die in a storm. But we have a fur coat, and we find a shack on the edge of the forest."

"Hang on a minute." He jumped up and disappeared down the hall. Shortly he returned carrying a plush sable coat, an open bottle of red wine and two glasses. "This coat belonged to my grandmother back before fur was politically incorrect." He filled the glasses with wine, rested the bottle on the hearth, then spread the coat over the rug. "Lie down."

Kay sank into the fur and gasped at the luxurious sensation. "Oh, my."

"You know," he said, "I've been going about this whole seduction the wrong way."

"How so?" she purred and rubbed her body into the coat like a kitten curling up to its mother.

"I've been doing to you what I thought would make you responsive."

"And you've been doing a damn fine job of it, too."

He shook his head. "I was off base. You need to learn what turns you on, to learn to control your own body before you turn it over to me." He sat down cross-legged beside her. "Let's get that dress off."

With incredible slowness that pushed her to the limits of endurance, he unbuttoned her dress and slipped it over her head. Her underwear was next. He unhooked her bra and tossed it into the corner. A second later her red satin thong followed. The fireplace gave off enough heat to warm her bare skin.

"Give me your hand," he said.

She did as he asked.

He took it, guided her hand to her belly. "Touch yourself."

"What?"

"Just do it."

"While you watch?"

His gray eyes had turned stormy slate. "Yes."

"I feel silly."

"Stop that thought right now. You're anything but silly. Have a sip of wine." He held the glass to her lips. Obediently she raised her head and swallowed the tepid liquid. "Good girl. Now close your eyes and let your fingers do the walking. Pretend you're alone. I'm not here.''

Hesitantly Kay traced her fingers over her breasts, amazed at how good it felt.

She was really embarrassed at first, but the more she let herself go, the more Quinn made appreciative noises. She loved hearing that she turned him on. She snuggled into the fur coat and tugged at her nipples. When she twisted gently, they came to life. A warm, wonderful tingling spread from her belly to her thighs. She followed the sensation with her hands.

She could hear Quinn's breathing, and his raspy intake of air spurred her on. She caressed herself and slowly slid one finger into her folded flesh. This felt great, but lonely. She wanted to see Quinn. Opening her eyes, she was shocked and yet thrilled to find him naked and hard.

Quinn had never watched a woman pleasure herself, and it was driving him beyond insane. He'd done well to hold on this long.

''Help me,'' she whispered. ''I don't want to do this by myself.''

Yes! He surged toward her, came to rest beside her on the fur coat. He began by kissing her and took his time working his way down to her other pair of lips. When he ventured too close to her delicate cleft, she hissed in her breath.

Easy, he told himself, easy. That pretty pink cleft was a shy little devil. Gently he wet her with his mouth and when he pulled away, she moaned.

He retrieved the lubricants he'd bought for her, moistened his fingers with a smooth gel and rubbed them across her blood-engorged flesh. With the first two fingers of his right hand he carefully edged them apart.

Starting directly to the left of her pulsating cleft and inching clockwise, he brushed against her with fast, short, circular stokes, looking for the perfect combination that would rocket her to the moon.

So as not to abrade her tender membranes, he made sure her cleft stayed wet and slick by dipping his fingers into her warm recesses and drawing out a trail of love juices to rub over her burgeoning womanhood.

The small cleft changed as her arousal reached new heights. It swelled, grew harder and finally climbed eagerly from its hooded cave.

"I don't want to hurt you," he whispered, "or ruin your arousal. Show me what feels good to you. Talk to me. Tell me."

She brought her hand to his. He followed her lead, memorized her every move. It was the most intimate thing he'd ever indulged in with anyone.

"Oh, Quinn," she breathed, and writhed beneath him. "Yes. Right there. Like that."

His own arousal was beyond anything he'd ever felt before. Together they massaged and stroked and caressed her, both working in tandem to achieve the same goal. But after forty minutes, Kay still wasn't anywhere near the summit. Maybe it was because she was too nervous about having him watch her.

Then he had an idea. It was something he'd heard once, supposedly a favorite sexual trick of Marilyn Monroe's. It would solve the problem of Kay's embarrassment and yet allow her to have full control over her own orgasm. It was worth a try. If it didn't work, well…

Since their relationship had no foundation other than

a physical one, Quinn didn't even want to think about that. He would present her with what she so desperately craved. He would, he would, he would.

Kay whimpered in frustration. "I'm so close," she moaned. "Why can't I get there?"

"You will, baby," he soothed. "You will. I promise. Keep stroking, I'll be right back."

Kay almost burst into tears the minute Quinn left the room. She had a feeling he was at his wit's end. She bit down hard on her bottom lip. Everything he'd done for her felt so good. He'd treated her like a princess—she couldn't let him down. If she had to, she'd fake the orgasm for his sake.

"Get off the coat," he commanded.

She rolled over and looked up at him. He had a plastic tarp under one arm and a bottle of baby oil in his hand. His erection was still as big as the state of Alaska. He took the coat from the rug and tossed it on the couch. Then he spread the tarp across the rug.

"What's going on?"

"Shh." He began coating the front of her body in baby oil. "Now," he said, when he'd finished, "you oil up my back."

He lay facedown on the tarp. Puzzled, Kay took the bottle of heated oil and squirted some onto his back. He groaned deeply as she ran her hand along his naked torso, down his buttocks and legs until he was as wet with oil as she was. She loved the feel of his firm skin beneath her fingers.

"Now what?" she asked when she'd finished the task.

"Lie on top of me."

This was a weird request. Feeling awkward, she lay

down atop him, her breasts smashed flat against his shoulder blades.

"Your breasts feel like velvet," he murmured.

"Your back is so muscular. Hard as a rock." She breathed into his ear.

"I'm going to stay completely still. This is all you, babe. You're at the helm. You're in control."

"But what do I do?"

"Slide your hands down my arms."

She wasn't sure what was going on, but she enjoyed feeling the wide expanse of his back beneath her, and she trusted him. She raised herself enough to lean forward, clasp her hands around his wrists and slip her arms down the length of his.

It felt like the time she went shooting over that Slip-and-Slide with the maid's kids.

"That's right. Keep touching, keep moving," he coached. "Make love to my back. You're looking for a certain spot. Go down a little."

Spurred by the easy glide from the baby oil, she got into the rhythm, rode on the motion. She rocked her hips in slow, small circles pressing her pubic bone directly against his tailbone.

And then she found it. The spot on his body that was a perfect fit for her cleft to snuggle into. A nice, welcoming groove.

She let loose with a shout of glee and wriggled happily.

Nothing had ever felt so good. She kept rocking, stoking her own fire. Her aching cleft set the pace, as she rubbed it up and down, up and down his oil-soaked skin. Up and down and around and around. She surfed his body like a wahine cruising a curl off Oahu's north shore.

"Quinn!" she cried, desperate to share her experience with the big, motionless man beneath her. "This feels phenomenal."

"Go, baby, go. Get it anyway you can."

"I'm getting so close. I can taste it rising up in my throat."

She clasped her arms around his waist, squeezed him tight. His heart was pounding so loudly she could feel it vibrating throughout his whole body and up into hers.

"Glory!" he cried, startled at the extreme intimacy this unorthodox maneuver wrought. "I can feel every twitch you make, Kay."

"Quinn, it's happening. I'm coming."

And then it hit her with the force of an oncoming freight train. Her entire body was engulfed in a hot, flushed, quaking release that started in her sensitive cleft but unfurled in a jerking starburst all the way to her toes.

She shuddered as wave after wave crashed into her. It was a force more powerful than an erupting volcano, more awe-inspiring than an ageless glacier. It was as if every dam in the country had broken at once, spewing torrents of wild water over the land. Seven days of sweet torture, years of hungry fantasies, a lifetime of repression burst forth from her.

At last! At long last!

Panting, she slid off Quinn's back. He rolled over, tucked her into the curve of his arm and smiled down at her. "My only regret," he whispered, "was not being able to see your face."

She was dishrag limp and unable to speak for a good five minutes. When she finally caught her breath, all she could say was, "That was…incredible."

In that fortuitous moment Quinn's telephone rang.

He leaned in to kiss her. She raised her head.

The phone rang again.

"Are you going to answer that?" she murmured sleepily, his lips so close the air vibrated off his mouth back to hers as she spoke.

"Let the machine pick up." He lightly ran his tongue over her upper lip.

By the time the machine intercepted the call, her arms were entwined around his neck, her legs around his waist, and their lips were fused.

"Quinn, this is your mother. Are you home? If you're home, please pick up."

"You better answer that," Kay said into his mouth.

"Do I have to?"

"It might be important."

Sighing, Quinn untangled Kay's limbs and got to his feet. "I'm here, Ma," he said, picking up the receiver and running a hand through his hair. His gaze slid over to his sexy Kay and he winked at her. "What's up?"

"Liam is rushing Candy to the hospital in Juneau. It looks like she might be in preterm labor. Your father's been at the station all day, and I need him at home. My ankle is giving me fits. Is there any way you can sub for Liam tonight?"

"Right now?"

"Yes, dear. Meggie's at the station for now, but Liam and Candy want her to fly with them."

Quinn took a deep breath. He loved his family and he was distressed to learn that Liam and Candy were having a crisis, but tonight of all nights? When he'd promised Kay he would make love to her?

He glanced at Kay again. She'd gotten to her feet

and was looking at him with a quizzical expression on her face.

Helplessly he met Kay's gaze. "I gotta go," he muttered, holding a palm over the phone so his mother couldn't hear. "Minor emergency."

Kay nodded.

"Okay, I'll be right there," he told his mother.

"You're a good son."

He told her goodbye, hung up and gave his attention to Kay.

"I hope everything's all right," she said.

Briefly he explained what was happening. "I'm so sorry," he apologized. "I intended for us to spend the whole night together."

"Hey, it's not your fault." She shrugged. "There'll be other nights."

"But you're leaving on Saturday."

"And this is only Sunday. Go. Help out your family."

"You're sure?"

"Don't be silly, of course I'm sure."

Her forgiveness and easy understanding filled him with an odd sensation. When he first met her, he'd been attracted to her physically, but he'd thought that was as far as the attraction went. In all honesty, he'd seen her as a spoiled, rich socialite. But here she was acting anything but spoiled. And in that moment Quinn knew his attraction had jumped to a whole new level.

13

HOW COULD SHE get upset with Quinn, even though her body was aching for his attention? Devotion to his family was one of his most attractive traits. She loved that his family meant so much to him, that they were so close. She wished his family was hers. She wished she could be a part of such a loving community.

In six days, she would be gone. His family was here for a lifetime. How could she begrudge him his choice?

She didn't, but as she watched him shrug into his coat, she couldn't seem to tamp down the torrent of loneliness washing through her.

Alone again.

Alone and super horny. She wanted more sex. More orgasms. More of him.

"Stay here," Quinn instructed, coming over to brush her lips lightly with his. "I'll be back after midnight. Eat some supper, watch a movie, finish off that glass of wine, take a nap, but don't you dare go anywhere. Got that? We're not through yet."

She nodded, even though a nagging voice in the back of her head was urging her to go to the bed-and-breakfast, pack her things and head back to New York right now. They'd yet to take that irrevocable step toward becoming full-fledged lovers. This was her chance to back out before she made a fool of herself. Before she got seriously hurt.

Because she was already starting to care for Quinn far more than was prudent.

"Say it." He leaned over to nibble on her earlobe. "Say you'll be waiting here for me when I get home."

What was it about this man? He seemed to know every errant thought that passed her mind. How? She had spent so much of her life learning to cloak her feelings, keep her countenance unreadable, her head clear, her mind undisturbed, and yet she could never fool Quinn. What gave her away? she wondered. How had he known she was panicking?

His gentle nipping of her earlobe was more than she could bear. "I'll be here," she promised huskily. "Now go."

"I could get used to this," he said. "Having you to come home to."

Kay inhaled sharply. "It's not me you want, Quinn. It's a wife."

He stepped back a moment, studied her in the foyer light. Too bad she couldn't read his mind the way he seemed to read hers.

"Yeah," he said. "You're right. Long term, I do want a wife, but for tonight..." His gaze raked over her body. "I can't forget what sizzling, sexy blonde will be waiting for me."

He turned and walked out the door, leaving Kay feeling more confused than ever. She wandered about the house, snooping a little and finally ending up in the large room upstairs where he'd taken her the night he'd shown her the northern lights.

She didn't open any closets or drawers, but she did

touch the things that were lying out. His ice skates, the blades cleaned and freshly sharpened. His gloves. His heavy snow boots—good grief, he wore a size fourteen. She fingered his hockey jersey, which she held to her nose to breathe in the scent of him. The smell aroused her with a perplexing kick to the belly. Immediately she dropped the jersey back on the chair where she had found it.

She drifted over to the stereo system, flicked on the radio, then settled herself on the couch with her wine to watch the show outside the window. The northern lights were in full swing, flickering and dancing hypnotically.

''Hello, listeners.'' The soothing sound of Quinn's voice came through the speakers and wrapped around her like a thermal blanket. ''You're listening to KCRK, number 840 on your AM dial. Sorry folks, but you're stuck with the native son tonight. Mack's flying Liam and Candy into Anchorage as we speak. Seems little Liam Junior is trying to put in his appearance two and a half months too early. I know they'll appreciate any prayers you can send the family's way.''

A knot formed in Kay's throat. Bear Creek was such a caring community. Small, intimate, cozy, a place where neighbors looked out for one another and nobody worried about stupid, inconsequential things like what kind of wine went with what kind of meal, or which pair of earrings to wear to an art-gallery opening.

Kay realized she'd invested too much of her life worrying about things that didn't really matter.

''On a lighter note,'' Quinn was saying, ''Millie Peterson and Doodles are doing just fine. Millie's staying with her sister over in Haines for a while in case anyone wants to run by and say hi. And thanks to everyone who donated money and clothes. Also, I'd like to thank everyone for helping out our visitor from New York City, Kay Freemont, with her article on Bear Creek. The magazine will be hitting the newsstands in mid-May, so be sure and drop by Leonard Long Bear's to get your copy."

Kay grinned at the radio, brought her wineglass to her lips and took a sip.

"And speaking of Kay, I'd like to dedicate this next song to her."

Rod Stewart's "Hot Legs" soon issued forth.

Kay hooted her approval and started tapping a foot in time to the lively music. After it was over, Quinn came back on. "It's an open request line tonight, folks. So call in—577-5555 for those of you with bad memories—and let me know what you'd like to hear tonight."

Getting to her feet, Kay padded back downstairs, took her cell phone from her purse and punched in the numbers to the radio station.

"I'd like to request a song," she said.

"Yes, ma'am, what can I play for you?" He gave no hint that he knew it was her, but how could he not know?

"'Natural Woman' by Aretha Franklin. Do you have that one?"

"Why, yes, ma'am, I believe we do."

She grinned again, sat down in front of the fire and kept the cell phone in her lap. She hummed along with the song that expressed her sentiments exactly. Quinn did make her feel like a natural woman. Sexy, feminine, loving.

"We gotta another dedication, folks," he said, when "Natural Woman" was over. Then he played a very provocative Barry White number, and Kay knew he was playing that one for her as well.

It was naughty, suggestive, and Barry's deep-throated voice sent spikes of hot desire down her spine. Damn! At this rate she wasn't going to last until midnight, which was when the radio station went off the air and Quinn returned home.

Kay felt herself go soft and moist and warm inside. She picked up her cell phone and dialed the station again. "How about 'You Sexy Thing'?"

"Coming right up," Quinn replied. He played her request followed by "You Can Leave Your Hat On."

That gave her an image to giggle about. She programmed the radio station to speed dial and whispered seductively when he answered, "'Let's Get It On.'"

"Your wish is my command."

Kay giggled again and pressed the back of her hand to her mouth.

He topped "Let's Get it On" with "Feel like Making Love."

"Keep those requests coming," Quinn said, when the song had played. "Oh, wait, I've got a call right now. Go ahead, caller."

"Hey!" Kay recognized the voice as that of old Gus. "Why don't you two have sex, already?"

Quinn sputtered into the microphone. "Er...I don't know what you're talking about. I've only been taking requests."

"Stop yanking my chain, Scofield. Obviously the

lady's hot for you, and the rest of us would like to listen to something a little less arousing. Play something decent, like big-band tunes.'' Gus huffed loudly, then disconnected.

Kay burst out laughing.

Quinn put on ''In the Mood,'' which only made her laugh harder. Why was she sitting here? Kay wondered. Why not toddle on over to the radio station and surprise him?

She grabbed the bottle of wine from the hearth where Quinn had left it, hurried into the kitchen, dug a wheel of cheddar cheese from the fridge and scooped a loaf of crusty sourdough bread off the counter.

Then, just before she put on his grandmother's fur coat, she took off her dress. Wearing nothing but stockings, garter belt, stilettos and the heavy sable coat, she got into the Wagoneer and drove to the radio station.

At nine-thirty, the main street of Bear Creek was deserted. Fat snowflakes spiraled from the pitch-black sky. The only vehicles she passed were the few trucks and cars gathered outside the Happy Puffin bar. Her heart hammered as she parked in front of the KCRK station. She could see Quinn through the window, seated in the booth, headphones over his ears.

The sight of him made her stomach go all jiggly.

Her breath came in frosty puffs. She knocked on the door, balancing precariously on her too-high heels, the bottle of wine in one arm, the cheese wheel and loaf of bread in the other.

A second later Quinn pulled open the door with such force he knocked her off balance, and she tumbled into his arms.

"Whoa." He grabbed her shoulders to steady her. "What are you doing out in this weather?"

"Coming to see you." She grinned up into his face. "I realized old Gus was right. It is high time we had sex, already. Real sex. Not just playing around."

"You called what we did earlier 'just playing around'?"

"Uh-huh. Now I'm ready for the hard stuff."

"Get in here." He tugged her inside and shut the door against the swirling cold. "Silly woman." He pressed her to his chest, breathed into her hair.

"I brought sustenance." She held out the wine and bread.

His eyes glimmered. "You're one hell of a woman, Kay Freemont, you know that?"

He parked her on a tweed couch in the studio. "Have a seat. I gotta go give the call letters and put on some more music. Got a request?"

"You pick." She smiled and settled back against the seat.

He did so in record time, the strains of Nat King Cole's "Unforgettable" seeping into the room. In his hands he held two paper cups. He appropriated the wine from where she'd set it on the floor, filled the cups and passed one to her.

"To the sexiest woman on the planet." He raised his glass.

"I can't drink to that. I'm not the sexiest woman on the planet."

"You are to me," he growled softly.

She drank then to the sexuality she'd repressed for so long. The sexuality that Quinn had so lovingly cultivated and coaxed from her over the course of the past eight days.

"I'm ready, Quinn," she said, finishing the wine and blinking in surprise at her sudden boldness. "No more games. I want you. Right here. Right now. Right this very minute."

GOD, BUT SHE WAS gorgeous, swaddled in his grandmother's fur coat with nothing showing but her legs from the calf down encased in crimson silk stockings. Her sweet feet were in sexy stiletto heels.

Her hair, normally perfectly controlled, was mussed, and her lipstick had come off on the edge of her paper cup.

He liked her this way. Relaxed. Natural. Asking for what she needed from him.

She was so beautiful and yet so out of place here on the worn tweed couch in his parents' radio station in Bear Creek, Alaska. She deserved to have her first orgasms at the Plaza Hotel in New York City while dining on chocolate-covered strawberries and expensive champagne, not supping on stale sourdough bread and third-rate wine. She deserved so many things he couldn't provide.

She reached out a finger, ran it along the crease cleaving his forehead. "Stop worrying," she murmured. "Everything's going to be all right."

But was it?

Quinn studied her, knowing she didn't belong here, knowing he had no right to want her as badly as he did. She was on the rebound, after all, looking for sex as a way to rebuild her self-esteem. He was a vehicle to her goal, and although he couldn't blame her for that, he couldn't seem to stop himself from wanting more.

Take what you can get. When the ad comes out in the magazine, you'll be knee-deep in women and Kay will be nothing but a pleasant memory. Make the most of it.

"Let me just make sure we're not interrupted." He went to the door and slipped the lock into place with a resounding click. He flicked off the overhead fluorescent bulb, leaving them bathed in the glow of red and green lights from the control panel.

Her almond eyes widened, and she ran the tip of her tongue along her lips, making him hotter than the volcanic Ring of Fire bubbling beneath Alaska's crust.

She was like Alaska itself. A cool, perfect beautiful exterior with a hot, smoldering center just waiting to erupt. He'd sensed this about her from the moment he'd seen her on the plane.

And her exciting combination of fire and ice stirred something inside him, just as his homeland did.

He admired so many things about her. The way she carried herself, regal and self-confident. The little noises she made when he caressed her. The taste of her mouth. Her unexpected laughter, her inquisitive mind, the special smile she gave him when he'd pleased her.

How he loved making her smile. He was ready to please her any way he could. All night long.

Kay shifted on the couch. She lounged against the armrest, swung her legs across the cushions until she was sprawled out provocatively. Her teeth sank into her bottom lip as he sauntered nearer.

He grinned wickedly, and his fingers went to the

buttons of his flannel shirt. Kay sat up straighter, her eyes riveted to his fingers, watching as, one by one, he undid the buttons and stripped off the shirt.

Next came his sweater, then his T-shirt and at last his thermal top. When his chest was completely exposed, Kay's mouth dropped open and she rubbed the back of a hand across her forehead.

He winked, stepped closer. He was almost to the couch, his clothes strewn in a haphazard path behind him. Looking at her made him hungry all over again. And this time not for bread and wine, but for a taste of that sumptuous skin. He licked his own lips.

Yum.

Kay's gaze traveled from his chest to his mouth and remained transfixed on his lips. Enjoying himself immensely, Quinn rounded the couch and slowly lowered himself beside her, his blue-jeaned thigh brushing against her stiletto heel. He watched the pulse at the base of her throat jump, felt a corresponding surge of blood through his body.

Tonight his goddess was going to come during intercourse. Tonight she'd be screaming his name in reverence.

He leaned across her legs, her knees hitting him midchest, the crush of fur against his nipples. He idly toyed with a strand of her hair, then oh-so-gradually traced his finger down her right ear.

She shivered.

Violently.

And closed her eyes. He watched the column of her throat work as she swallowed.

"What," he whispered, "are you wearing beneath that coat?"

"Why don't you see for yourself?" she invited.

His finger tracked a path from her ear to her cheek to her chin, then slid down that hot, hot throat to her collarbone, where he parted the fur coat, splayed his hand beneath it and found nothing but bare skin.

And he'd thought he had a raging hard-on before. That erection felt puny compared to this shaft of steel rising from him now. If he didn't watch himself, this whole endeavor would be over in a matter of seconds.

He pushed his hand farther down, relishing in the feel of her silken flesh. He peeled back the coat, watched his man-size fingers glide over her smooth breasts. He inhaled as deeply as she when his thumb rasped over her nipple and he cupped the full globe, bent his head to kiss it, then looked up to meet her gaze.

Her eyes were glazed, her breathing thready.

"You look more delicious than red-velvet cake, sweetheart. I could eat you right up with my hands tied behind my back."

"Oh, Quinn, you say the nicest things to me."

"I mean what I say, Kay. I'm not a man who tap-dances around the truth."

"And I love that about you."

"Honesty can make a guy unpopular at times."

"Not with me. I find it refreshing."

"I find you refreshing." His eyes gobbled her up. Strangely his heart felt too big for his chest.

"Nobody's ever appreciated me the way you do."

"By nobody, I'm assuming you mean that sorry son-of-a-dog you used to date."

Kay nodded.

"Forget about him," Quinn growled. "He was a

jerk and he didn't have any idea what a treasure he threw away. I appreciate you, darling. And don't you ever forget it."

"Don't," she said, her voice oddly choked, "be so nice to me."

"Why not?"

"Because if you're nice, I'll want to stay, and we both know I don't belong here."

He said nothing to that because he wanted to beg her to stay. But Bear Creek had nothing to offer a blue-blood magazine reporter from the most cosmopolitan city in the world. He could offer her no more than this. If Alaska hadn't been enough for Meggie, who'd been born and raised here, how could it be enough for Kay? Most women, his sister included, considered Alaska a lonely place. He had no right even to ask her to stay. None at all. He was going to take what he could have and give her a night to cherish always.

"Let's not talk anymore," she said huskily. "Let's just make love. Send me into orbit, big guy. I want to know what it feels like to frolic with the aurora borealis."

Quinn wrapped his arms around her narrow waist, then leaned back against the opposite end of the couch and pulled her on top of him, until they were touching head to toe, her bare breasts flattened against his bare chest, the warm apex of her womanhood flush against the zipper of his jeans.

She let out a low, feral sound that inflamed him beyond measure. She nuzzled her face in his neck and whispered his name.

His hands skimmed down her luscious body, then back up again beneath the plush material of the fur coat. He kissed her throat, then licked and lightly sucked because he couldn't get enough of the taste of her.

He rubbed her calves through the silky material of her stockings, and it was almost his undoing. He fondled the backs of her knees, then toyed with the garter at her thigh. His hands roamed higher, kneading the tight muscles of her compact tush until he was hot as a blowtorch and hard as the arctic tundra.

How was he going to last long enough to give her the pleasure she needed? The top of his head was going to blow off if he didn't get some relief soon.

Kay writhed above him. "Quinn, you make me so wild. I never knew I could lose control the way I do with you."

"Wild women wanted," he murmured, repeating the tag line of his ad copy. He slid his fingers down between her thighs, found her wet and hot. "Are you wild for me, Kay?"

"Wild, savage, frantic."

"That's good. 'Cause I'm going to have to make love to you now, darling, or go insane."

HE WAS BEYOND handsome to her. Beyond strength and size and manliness. He was clean and raw and unspoiled. He was pure man and pure animal. He and his instincts, his ancestry, blended together against all the edicts of the polite society from whence she came, and Kay loved him for that.

His mouth claimed hers. Roughly, sweetly. He tasted of heat and wine and soul. He smelled of Sitka spruce, wood smoke and lemony soap.

The life she'd always lived to satisfy the needs of

her civilized culture was erased, as he framed her face with both hands and stared deeply into her eyes.

The pressure in her very center that had been building night after night was coiled tight, waiting to burst forth again in sweet release.

"Straddle me," he whispered, gently pulling his lips from hers. "I want you to be in control. You need it this way."

She arranged her thighs on either side of him. She felt the hard bulge of his erection throb against his pants, against her bottom. Her hands fumbled frantically with his belt, unbuckling it and jerking it through the loops with a slithering swish. She grabbed for the metal button, but was trembling so hard she couldn't free it from the buttonhole.

"Let me."

She shifted, rising on her knees and leaning her right side into the back of the couch. He raised his hips, undid the button, tugged down the zipper and shucked both his pants and underwear at the same time, shimmying them past his hips.

Kay took it from there. Grabbing the denim and his long johns, she pulled the garments off his legs and tossed them aside. Panting, she returned her attention to him, and her eyes widened as she surveyed the long, hard length of him, getting her first really good look at his impressive package.

When she'd dubbed him Paul Bunyon that first day on the plane, she hadn't been far off the mark.

She stared, openmouthed. "You're incredible."

"You're not so bad yourself, sweetheart."

"I've got to have some of that." She swung her

legs over his torso again, her body clenching in anticipation of riding his erection into oblivion.

"Wait," he said in a strangled voice, and struggled to sit up.

"What?" She stared. Dazed, glazed, starving beyond measure.

"I don't have a condom," he croaked. "They're back at my place."

Her face broke into a smile as she slipped her hand into her pocket and produced a small foil packet. "Let me deal with this one, fireman."

Then with the inexpert fumbling of a woman who'd researched and written about such tricks but never tried them herself, Kay scooted down until she was sitting on his knees. She placed the condom in her mouth, leaned forward and, after a few failed attempts, successfully rolled it over his shaft.

Quinn groaned and shuddered so hard she thought he was going to come right then and there. "Give me a minute, sweetheart."

She sat up, watched his face as he fought for control.

"Okay." He held out his hands to her. "Come back up here."

With the fur coat slapping seductively against her naked behind, she straddled him once more, facing forward. Remembering all those sexy tomes she'd read, Kay curled her hand around his shaft and slid him into the length of her.

She spread her hot wetness across the head of him, then lowered herself, impaled herself just half an inch, no more, then pulled up again. She rubbed her yearning cleft all over his swollen end, then let him slide a little deeper. She pulled away again.

And repeated the steps several times until, desperately, he grabbed her around the waist and yanked her down hard until her tight, wet, warmth engulfed his flaming erection.

Simultaneously they hissed in their breaths as they were fully joined for the first time.

Quinn was rigid as a slab of marble beneath her, his hands spanning her waist, his face twisted in a grimace of pure pleasure. He penetrated her, filled her up, filled the emptiness that had been inside her for so many years. Filled her beyond her knowledge of herself. She had never been so physically possessed.

Peals of pleasure unfolded and sang through her blood. She moved with him as if she'd been doing it all her life. Moved as graceful as horse and rider. Up and down. Agonizingly slowly at first, getting her bearings, adjusting to the thickness of him. She stretched out on top of him, her legs over his, her face cradled against his neck. She rocked her hips, pushing lower and lower until her cleft pressed directly against the base of his shaft.

"That's it, sweetheart, that's it," he encouraged. "Take charge. It's your turn to be in the driver's seat."

She reveled in her ability to do this for him, and she gave a cry of joy at the mystery of her woman's magic, which allowed her to accommodate his maleness. She sat up, squatted over him, feet planted precariously in the yielding couch cushions just outside his thighs, hands on his chest for balance.

In an instant she was flying. Riding up to the tingling tip of him, then pounding back down. Every smack of her bottom against his hips produced in him the most erotic groans she'd ever heard.

He was close to jettisoning off the edge of reason. She heard it in his voice. Not yet. Not yet.

She stopped, then turned carefully, keeping him embedded inside her as she moved. She leaned her back against his chest, begged him to reach around and caress her breasts. She pulled her legs together on top of him and squeezed, the muscles of her thighs and buttocks effectively became a velvet vise around his manhood.

"Kay," came his muffled, garbled cry, and she felt an awesome sense of power. "I'm about to come."

"Hold on. There's more."

She knelt over his hips and leaned forward. She knew for him this was an incredibly erotic position. He had a spectacular view of her bouncing bottom. He could actually watch himself slip in and out of her.

Instinct urged her to quicken the pace, and soon she was thumping him so hard the couch vibrated. Soon, it seemed, the whole room was vibrating, singing with heat and energy and the dark pulsating power that emanated from the frenzied meeting of their bodies. Kay worried crazily that the small room couldn't hold the blizzard force of their grappling union.

"Unforgettable," Nat King Cole sang for the umpteenth time.

Kay felt both exalted and afraid. Her body was a glorious temple and he, Quinn, exalted her.

And that's when she flew apart.

A tingly, heated buzz that started inside the deepest, wettest part of her and rushed forth to encompass every nerve ending, every cell.

She came. Hard.

It was explosive. The twisted emotions of a lifetime

came pouring out of her. The frustration, the shame, the avoidance of intimacy all evaporated.

She was laughing, she was crying. Tears streaked her face, giggles shook her body. She'd done it! She'd had an orgasm during intercourse! She felt like the queen of the world. And Quinn was her king.

I'm not frigid, Lloyd. I'm not. You were wrong. So damned wrong about me.

She gasped, slid off him, turned around and collapsed against his chest. She'd always hoped it could be like this. Hoped and wished and prayed.

He wrapped his arms tightly around her, tenderly kissed her forehead, then brushed his fingers through her sweaty hair. "There, there, sweetheart. You did good."

"Thank you," she whispered, tears still choking her voice. "Thank you, thank you, thank you."

14

QUINN FELT PROUDER than he had the day he had scored a hat trick to beat the Ketchikan Freeze in intramural hockey play-offs. He had done it. He had helped Kay achieve the orgasms she so deeply deserved, and he had still managed to hang on to his control. He hadn't come, and he wasn't through with her yet.

But for the moment, he lay basking in his accomplishment, her head resting against his chest, his fingers entwined in her hair, her scent all around him, her sweet taste in his mouth. He lay listening to "Unforgettable" play on and on, past the time when the station should have signed off the air. But he wasn't about to get up and break this wondrous spell.

She'd taught him so much in a short period of time. How to be patient and tender and understanding. Unwittingly she'd shown him how to be a good husband, skills he would need when he found his life's mate. By teaching Kay about her own body, he'd learned serious self-control. He'd also learned to put her needs ahead of his own. He felt grateful for these lessons and forever indebted to her.

She was an extraordinary woman.

As he lay watching her breathe, he began to kiss her. She roused and met his gaze with a lusty gleam of her own.

"More?" she asked.

"Don't you know it?"

She purred deep in her throat. "Come here my burly bear of a man."

He treated her to more foreplay, then when she was once again fully aroused, he moved her around and entered her from behind, his belly against her back, one hand kneading her breasts and the other steadying her pelvis.

Kay flung back her hair and cried encouragement. Her frenzy excited him. Harder, faster he moved, driving deeper into her willing body.

When she said, "I can't bear any more, Quinn. I'm going to shatter into a million pieces," he knew the time had come. A second climax was upon her. He slipped his hand from her breasts to her protruding nub and rubbed with a gentle, ceaseless caress until he felt the beginning of her contractions.

"I'm coming, Quinn!" she cried.

He groaned.

Nothing had ever sounded so beautiful. Nothing had ever galvanized him as much as those words. Her cries pushed him over the edge, and he let his body's streaming heat launch him into oblivion.

Afterward they lay spent and content, suffused with well-being. They slept briefly. When they awoke, they talked of the sensations of their bodies, their physical desire for each other. Both avoided speaking of something deeper, of the emotions they were experiencing but afraid to express.

They reinvented kisses, warmed by the rhythmic blending of their breaths. No one had ever kissed like her. Kay's mouth traversed erotic areas he never knew he possessed—the nape of his neck, a sweet section of skin on the tender side of his upper arm, the back of his ear. He returned the favor, licking and nibbling in unusual spots.

They murmured to each other, lips muffled against breasts, throats, bellies. Neither of them spoke of the future or the past. Nothing existed but now.

They held each other, cuddled and spooned. They pulled the fur coat over their naked bodies and reveled in their new discoveries. Both were happier than they had ever been. Or so it seemed to Quinn.

SOMETIME AROUND FOUR in the morning, a steady pounding on the back door roused Kay from deep slumber.

"Hey," she whispered, poking Quinn gently in the ribs. "Someone's outside."

"Quinn," a woman called. "Are you in there? Is everything okay?"

Quinn grunted and sat up, blinking and yawning. His disheveled hair stood in spikes all over his head. "I feel like I've been trampled by Kong."

"There's some woman outside, knocking on the door," Kay said.

"Tell her to go away." He grinned. "I've got more woman than I can handle right here."

She pinched him lightly on the arm. "Don't get cute."

"Hey!" He rubbed the spot where she'd pinched, pretending it hurt. "You're vicious."

"Quinn!" the woman at the back door demanded. "Open up this minute or I'm gonna get J.C. to knock down this door."

"J.C.?" Kay clutched the fur coat to her bare breasts.

"Sheriff's deputy from over in Haines. But don't worry. Even though it's only five minutes by plane from here to Haines, it's eight hours by road. She's just making idle threats.

"Hang on, Meggie," Quinn called, searching the floor for his clothes. "I'll be right there."

He dressed, then pulled open the door, Meggie tumbled inside.

"My gosh, Quinn, what happened? Did you fall asleep or something?" Meggie shivered and stomped snow off her boots. "I just got back from taking Liam and Candy to the hospital. I drove by the station and saw your truck was still here and the Wagoneer, too. Then Mack called me and said that on his way home he had the radio tuned to KCRK and you were playing 'Unforgettable' over and over again. So I came here to see what gives."

"How's the baby?" Kay asked from her place on the couch.

"Oh," Meggie said, apparently noticing her for the first time. "You've got company." She wiggled her fingers in greeting. "Hi, Kay. Listen, I'm so sorry, I didn't mean to interrupt anything."

Grinning, Meggie started backing up.

"You didn't." Kay returned her smile. If her mother had taught her nothing else, it was how to make the best of awkward situations. "The baby?"

"Oh, they stopped Candy's contractions. Looks like Liam Junior's going to stay put until May, the way he's supposed to."

"That's great news," Kay said. "I'm glad to hear it."

"I'll just be going now." Raising a hand to her face

to hide her expanding grin, Meggie turned and rushed out the door.

"Guess we surprised her," Quinn said. While she and Meggie had been talking, he had given Nat King Cole a rest and signed off the radio station.

"Guess so."

He held out a hand to her. "Come on, sweetheart, let's go home."

LATER, IN QUINN'S four-poster, king-size bed, Kay lay looking up at the ceiling and listening to the reliable sound of his steady breathing.

He was sleeping on his stomach, one arm thrown around her waist, one leg pressed against hers. She loved that he wanted to touch her. Loved it and feared it.

Because as his body heated hers, his kindness, his tenderness, his unselfishness melted her heart. How had she grown accustomed to him so quickly? How had she come to anticipate his touch, to listen for the sound of his voice, to long for the flavor of his unique taste?

And how would she adapt when this was all gone? How could she ever be satisfied with her lonely New York apartment now?

He'd worked hard to give her a most precious gift. He'd held his own orgasm at bay, pushed his own needs aside for her. She'd never known a man like that. In fact, she had secretly doubted such men existed outside the pages of a romance novel.

But here he was. The man who'd taught her so much about herself.

Oh, the things he'd taught her.

Kay smiled into the darkness. His lips had branded

her in the most private of places, marking her as his own. And she'd not only let him, but begged him for more. He knew her body inside and out.

All she wanted to do was bask in the afterglow, revel in the glory of their lovemaking. But she was afraid of her escalating feelings for him. Worried that she might be falling in love.

You can't fall in love with him. It simply isn't prudent. He's from a different world. And besides, it's not really love. You're just infatuated. Grateful to him because he gave you the one thing that had eluded you for so long.

Sexual fulfillment.

No! her heart cried. It's not infatuation, it's something deeper, something more meaningful.

But her troubled mind, which for too long had been indoctrinated in staid thinking, wouldn't let her indulge such nonsense.

Okay, challenged her brain. *What if you* are *in love with him? There's no guarantee he loves you back.*

And even if he did love her back, she wasn't the kind of woman he needed. A man like Quinn needed a practical wilderness woman. A woman who could start her own fires and bake sourdough bread. A tough sort of woman who didn't turn blue in the cold and wasn't scared of a tame moose. He needed much more than a lover. He needed a companion and a friend. But most of all, he needed a woman who wasn't afraid of her feelings. A woman who could express her emotions and give herself to him wholly.

She could never be the kind of woman he needed. Never in a million years. If she'd learned anything from this adventure, she'd learned you have to be yourself. You can't pretend to be something you're not in order to please those around you.

She simply didn't have what it took to make it in Alaska. And the sooner she accepted that, the quicker she could start getting over him. Because deep in her heart, she knew that if she let herself, she could fall madly in love with him.

THEY AWOKE around noon on Thursday. They'd spent the past few days in bed, barely coming up for air, packing a lifetime of sexual memories in four short days. Good thing she'd already completed the research for her article. Quinn made blueberry pancakes, and then they bundled up and took a frosty walk through the forest, both of them revved into overdrive with excess energy from the long nights before.

In silence they tramped through woods muted with snow. Overhead a pair of bald eagles soared. They stopped for a few minutes and watched the regal creatures wing their way across the sky.

Quinn took her hand in his, helping her to step over fallen logs and frozen creekbeds. He marveled at how small and delicate her hand felt in his.

When they reached a clearing, she pulled away from him, took a deep breath and looked up at the gray, cloud-strewn sky, awash in only a modicum of pale yellow light. Her elegance and private nature never failed to stir him on an elemental level. She was so damned self-contained.

Somewhere along the way—maybe it was living in a big city with so much stimuli to block out, or maybe it came from putting on a game face for the high-society crowd she came from—she'd learned the art of withdrawing quietly into herself. Just another facet of her personality that drew him to her.

He admired the graceful way she moved and the way her mouth tipped up at the corners when she was pleased with him. He adored the way she blushed so easily at things he said or did, and the way she'd tilt her head in his direction when she was listening to him.

Face it, he told himself, making love to this woman had been a gigantic ego boost. He would never have believed a wilderness man from Bear Creek, Alaska, could attract the likes of Kay Freemont.

Somehow he'd managed to have done just that.

But soon she'd be leaving.

Leaving him alone with this empty space in his chest. Quinn didn't like that sensation. It made him feel helpless and vulnerable. And he hated feeling unprotected.

His emotions ran deep. So deep he was afraid to explore them. What if he actually spoke the word *love?*

You'd get hurt, stupid. That's what would happen.

Kay was rich, well-bred, classy. She would never move to Alaska, and the notion of him moving to New York was unfathomable. It was best not to speak of his feelings, to deny them even to himself. Despite the fact he'd spent the better part of the past two weeks trying to get her to express her feelings, he was not going to follow his own advice. His best bet was to simply live in the moment and stop thinking about the future. He'd always been good at that.

Sometime soon he'd find a wife, and he'd forget all about Kay Freemont.

Liar!

He would never forget her. Not if he lived to be a 108. She was unforgettable.

The tune played in his head and, damn, if an odd lump didn't rise in his throat.

"You look cold," he said to her. "Maybe we should go back."

"Okay," she said simply.

Then for no reason other than he wanted to nurture her, Quinn scooped her up in his arms and carried her back to the cabin. He took her upstairs to the bed and undressed her. They made love again, slow and leisurely.

Later, when he looked down into her face, he saw tears glistening in her eyes.

"What's wrong?" Sudden panic gripped him. "Did I hurt you?"

She gave him a watery smile. "Nothing," she whispered. "I'm just so happy."

He kissed the tears away, understanding immediately what she was feeling. Her tears tasted of her salty happiness. The happiness tinged with sorrow that this thing between them could never be more than it was right this moment.

He was the rebound guy. The tonic that gave her the strength to go forth and face the world again after being cheated on by her boyfriend. He'd served his purpose. He'd helped to heal her. That was enough.

Besides, tourist season was fast approaching, and he had a lot to do to get ready. They were adding new rafting trips to the itinerary for the cruise-ship excursions, and he had signed up to serve on the mountain-rescue squad once a week. And besides, he had a wife to find.

"I better go," she said. "I've got to finish my article. I checked my voice mail, and Judy's already left six panicked messages."

"Will I see you again before you leave Bear Creek?"

"I've got an early flight on Saturday morning, so Mack's flying me into Anchorage tomorrow night. I've booked a room in a motel near the airport."

"This is your last day, then." Amazing how they'd spent the past few days together without discussing the details of her departure. But they'd both been avoiding the inevitable, choosing not to speak of it until they absolutely had to.

"Yes."

"I'll come with you to Anchorage. We can share the room." He quirked a smile. "One last orgasm for the road."

THE LAST TIME they made love was bittersweet. Kay memorized everything. The way Quinn moved above her, the feel of his hands on her skin, the taste of him on her tongue. She imprinted the decor of the room, what they wore, the room-service meal they ate.

I'm making memories, she told herself. To sustain her through the hard days ahead. She had a lot to think about, a lot of soul-searching to do.

What did she want in her future? She knew one thing—she had to face Lloyd again, to confront him about how shabbily he'd treated her. Before she could move on, she needed that closure.

No one was going to believe the change in her.

But it was high time. And thanks to Quinn, she now had the courage to proceed with her life.

He sat holding hands with her in the terminal while the ramp workers de-iced the plane. Her heart lay heavy in her chest. A wave of feeling welled up in her, and she had to fight to keep from expressing it. He'd trained her too well. And there was so much she wanted to say, but the old Kay reminded her that silence sometimes was golden. She figured it was better to stay quiet and not tell him what she feared. Because what would he do with that information?

"I can't thank you enough," she said when boarding for her plane was announced. She stood up, and he rose to his feet beside her.

"Sweetheart, I didn't do anything but take the lid off the box." He smiled tenderly, ran a finger down her cheek. "You had it in you all along."

"Thank you for believing in me. No one else did."

"They didn't see in you what I saw."

"And what was that?" she asked breathlessly.

"Passion." His eyes met hers. "Fire beneath the ice. Heat simmering under that unruffled surface."

"I'm glad you're so perceptive."

"And I'm glad you picked me to help liberate you."

"If you're ever in Manhattan, please call me."

"And if you talk your boss into doing a follow-up story on the bachelors of Bear Creek, I'll pick you up at the airport."

"I'll put a bee in Judy's ear."

He took her hand. He started to say something, then hesitated.

Over the intercom, the gate agent announced last call for her flight.

"I gotta go," she whispered.

He pressed his forehead to hers, looked deeply into her eyes. "You take care, Kay, you hear?"

"Same to you, big man."

"Maybe I'll call you sometime."

"I'd like that."

She slung her carry-on bag over her shoulder and started for the jetway.

"Hey, Kay," he shouted as she reached the mouth of the jetway.

She turned, her heart hammering.

"Remember when I told you there's supposed to be a lot of sunspot activity this summer?"

"Yes."

"Mean's the aurora will be highly visible. Maybe as far away as New York. Plus, the aurora does strange things to radio signals. If you're lonesome some night, turn to KCRK. Maybe you'll hear a song that reminds you of our time together."

"I'll do that." Damn. She had to go before she burst into tears.

Luckily the flight attendant rescued her. "Please, ma'am, if you don't move along, we're going to have to shut the plane door without you."

"Bye." She waved gaily over her shoulder at Quinn, putting on her game face and pretending that her heart wasn't splitting in two.

THE ADVANCE COPY of the June issue of *Metropolitan* magazine arrived in his mailbox in mid-April with a short note from Kay stuck to the front cover.

"Hope you like how the ad and article turned out," she'd written in her elegant script. "My publisher was very pleased. See page 110."

That was it? His spirits plummeted. He flipped to page 110.

There was the advertisement and on the opposite page was Kay's article. "The Bachelors of Bear Creek

Beckon; But Are You Gutsy Enough to Become a Wilderness Wife?''

He read slowly, cherishing every word, knowing Kay had written them. In glowing terms she exalted all the bachelors and their little town. Quinn's chest filled with emotion when she lauded his skills as both a hockey player and a volunteer fireman.

She wrote of the stark beauty of the land, the soul-stealing majesty of the mountains, the water, the wildlife. She described the northern lights. She wrote about the fierce independence of the Alaskans, their old-fashioned values, their love of the land.

Pride filled Quinn's heart. For his home, for Kay, for his life in Alaska. Obviously she'd fallen in love with the place.

But then came the negatives. Cold and darkness. Moose freely roaming downtown streets. Wolves and bears lurking in the woods. Danger aplenty. No convenience stores. No movie theaters. No shopping centers. No restaurants. She wrote of Liam and Candy's baby scare, how the hospital was a long plane ride away. She wrote of the isolation. She wrote about the lonely sound of the wind whipping through the Sitka spruce on frozen winter nights.

And any hope Quinn had been holding out that she'd come back disappeared. Much as she might love Alaska, it was too different from anything she'd ever known. Asking her to move here would be like asking a salmon to sprout wings and fly, or asking an eagle to unhinge his feathers and dive into the depths of the ocean.

Their differences were what had attracted them to each other, but it was those differences that kept them apart. And the main reason he hadn't called her.

Many times over the course of the past six weeks, he would start to pick up the telephone. But on each occasion, his doubts held him back. He feared he wasn't good enough for her. He told himself she needed her space, needed time to get her life in order. Needed to see if what she felt for him was real or merely the result of him being the one to open her up to her own sexuality.

Hell, truth be told, he had no idea what she felt for him.

Besides, if he kept picking at the wound, his heart would never heal.

He closed the magazine. Closed his eyes. He could see her as plainly as if she was standing in front of him, cloaked in his grandmother's fur coat and nothing else.

She was the sexiest, smartest, most savvy woman he'd ever known, and he'd been lucky to have her in his life even for a short while.

But he couldn't stop thinking about her. Since her visit, he'd lost ten pounds, because without her, food had no taste. He couldn't sleep—the bed seemed too empty, so he threw himself into getting ready for the tourist season. He'd added a whole new wilderness adventure to his regular offerings. The business kept him occupied from six in the morning to very late at night. That was the point. To stay so busy he had no time to think of her.

Except it wasn't working.

Quinn couldn't comb her from the snarl of his thoughts. No one smelled as good as Kay. No one he knew spoke with her smooth, polished voice. No one had her sleek hairstyle, her dynamic way of walking.

She was special and he was never going to find anyone else like her, so he might as well stop trying and start concentrating on what he could have. Like the cute new guide he'd hired last week. Or any of the women who would undoubtedly show up when *Metropolitan* hit the newsstands in May.

Except he couldn't seem to work up the energy even to think about dating.

Good grief, he thought suddenly. Was this more than mere infatuation? Could he actually be in love with Kay Freemont?

15

QUINN.

How she missed him, Kay thought as she sat in her office staring at page 110 of the June issue, which had come out in May and had been on the stands for three weeks now. Her gaze riveted on one of the four bare-chested bachelors stretched out like movie idols.

With a heavy sigh she traced a finger over his one-dimensional image and recalled what it felt like to touch him in the flesh. All sinew and muscle. All hard edges and solid tissue.

She thought about his winsome smile, his self-confident stance, the tender way he gazed at her when he didn't think she was looking. She thought of his loving family, his good-hearted, down-to-earth friends.

Since coming home to her own family, she'd been doubly struck by how shallow and image-conscious they were. Lloyd had begged her to come back. Her father had demanded she reconsider his proposal. Her mother had clucked her tongue and told her she was no longer behaving in a manner becoming of a Freemont. And when she finally spoke her mind—letting loose with a stream of opinions she'd kept cloaked for twenty-seven years, opinions that differed vastly from Charles and Honoria's rigid rules of conduct—they'd told her they didn't want to see her again until she had come to her senses.

Kay had told them not to hold their breaths.

That's when Kay realized exactly how much she had changed.

She no longer cared that her father was angry or that her mother was upset. She didn't care if Lloyd got his nose out of joint or if her mother's friends were furiously whispering gossip behind their hands. She was ready to make her own way, lead her own life, unfettered by the expectations of others.

Those two weeks in Alaska had transformed her.

Two weeks in Quinn's arms enjoying orgasm after orgasm and learning how to take control of her life.

"Knock, knock," Judy called from the doorway before strolling into Kay's office, a manila envelope tucked under her arm. An ear-to-ear grin split her face.

"Hi." Kay managed a smile.

"Guess what?"

"I'm not in the mood for guessing games, Judy."

"Still pining over the Mighty Quinn?"

"No." But even to her own ears, the denial rang false.

"Liar. But cheer up, I've got fabulous news." Her boss perched on the edge of her desk.

"I'm listening."

"Between the Bear Creek bachelors, your article and the contest, sales of our June edition are already up sixteen percent."

"You're kidding!" Kay gaped.

"Nope. And as a result, Hal's not only giving you a tidy bonus, but he's prepared to offer you the position of head writer when Carol leaves next month." Judy clapped her hands.

"That's nice."

"Nice? Is that all you're going to say? Kay, this is an opportunity of a lifetime."

What Judy said was true. Kay had dreamed of being head writer ever since she graduated from Vassar and hired on at *Metropolitan*. But somehow it no longer seemed like such a big deal.

"You're going to take the position, aren't you?"

Kay shrugged. "I don't know."

Judy stared at her. "You've been acting downright weird ever since you got back from Alaska."

"I've changed the way I look at things."

"Yeah, you've taken several steps backward. You used to be so focused, so centered, so ambitious. What happened?"

What had happened indeed?

She'd learned a new way of being. She'd learned to listen for the cries of bald eagles soaring overhead. She'd learned to enjoy the sight of moose trotting down the main street. She'd learned to love a place where the northern night sky lit up in a dancing swath of colored lights.

Unmindful of Judy's presence, Kay reached out to caress the photograph she'd framed on her desk. The picture Meggie had taken of her with the four bachelors at the Scofields' party and mailed to her when she'd gotten them developed. They'd even exchanged a few e-mails since then, but Meggie only mentioned Quinn in passing, and Kay had been reluctant to come right out and ask direct questions about him.

In the photo Quinn was standing to her left, Jake to

her right. Quinn's arm was draped over her shoulder, and he was gazing at her with a tender expression on his face.

"Oh, my God!" Judy exclaimed suddenly. "It's all so clear. Why didn't I see it before? You've been moping around here for weeks like a sick puppy. You're in love with the lumberjack."

Kay's head jerked up. "I'm not," she denied.

"Oh, yes, you are."

"Don't be ridiculous. Quinn and I were just..." What? Friends? No sir. Considering the sexual adventures they'd shared, they were so much more than that. Lovers? Well, not really. The word implied a long-term relationship. Two ships that passed in the night?

"Yes?" Judy arched an eyebrow, waited expectantly for her to continue.

"We had a good time together, but that's all it was."

"You sure about that? Your article was great. Full of emotion. You've never written anything so passionate," Judy enthused. "And you showed both sides of the coin. The sexy bachelors, that homey little town, the beauty of Alaska versus the serious negatives. Any woman that snags one of those guys can't say she wasn't forewarned."

Kay nodded.

"I was thinking, in case any of those bachelors does get married as a result of the article, maybe we could do a follow-up story. Would you like to go back?"

"I...I don't know." She would love to go back, but what if one of those bachelors was Quinn? Could she stand to see him with his new bride, his face shining with a happiness that had eluded them?

"Just think about it," Judy said. "In the meantime I brought these for you to look at. Thought you might enjoy picking the winning contest entry." She handed Kay the fat manila envelope.

"Thanks." Kay put the envelope in her top desk drawer. "Anything else?"

"No, that's all." Judy turned to go, but stopped when she reached the door. "Kay, if you really are in love with this man, don't let him go without a fight."

SEVERAL HOURS LATER Kay carried the manila envelope in her briefcase as she walked swiftly down a side street in the misting rain. She'd been late leaving work after a powwow with Hal about the possibility of taking over Carol's job as head writer. She'd tried for a taxi, but getting a cab in rainy weather was like getting good Chinese take-out in Bear Creek.

She'd gone through the bulk of contest entries Judy had given her, and while several were well written, none had jumped out at her. She had a few more to read, so she was bringing the rest home with her. But she couldn't really concentrate on the contest. Her thoughts were on Quinn, and she allowed her usual mindfulness to slip. She didn't even notice that she was the only person on the block, and when she passed a Dumpster, she didn't even look behind it.

Big mistake.

A man grabbed her from the shadows and held a knife to her neck.

Kay was so startled she couldn't even scream. Her brain went numb.

"Give me your purse, lady," the man demanded. "And the briefcase."

This simply could not be happening to her again. Mugged for the third time in as many years!

Resigned, she handed him her purse. But the clasp on her briefcase hung on her purse strap. He snatched at her things while at the same time throwing her to the ground. The briefcase burst open, and the manila folder fell to the ground beside her. The man ran off into the night, leaving Kay alone in the wet darkness bleeding from scrapes on her palms and knees.

It was almost midnight by the time she arrived home from the police station.

She plunked the manila envelope wearily on her bed. Her hometown. The place of her birth suddenly seemed like an alien and hostile place. Outside the window she heard the wail of an ambulance.

If only she had someone she could talk to. Someone who understood. She thought of Quinn.

Call him.

But what would she say? How would she begin? She wandered over to the radio, turned it to 840 AM as she'd been doing almost every night since she'd returned from Alaska. Even with her high-power radio, she'd picked up KCRK only a couple of times, and neither time had Quinn been manning the control booth.

She got nothing but a few staticky crackles. Glumly she sat on the bed. The manila envelope had torn during the encounter with the mugger, and one of the remaining contest entries was poking out. Idly Kay reached for it.

> I want to go Alaska because I'm very timid, and more than anything in the world I long to be brave. If Alaska can't save me, nothing can.

The heartfelt words reached out to Kay. The writer had touched something inside her. She, too, had gone to Alaska seeking salvation. And she'd found it. But in the end, she'd been too scared to act on her instincts. She hadn't trusted herself. Or her true feelings.

She glanced at the name on the entry form. Cammie Jo Lockhart from Austin, Texas.

"Well, Cammie Jo," Kay whispered. "Let's see if you can do better than I did. This is your chance to test your courage. You win the contest."

She closed her eyes and leaned back. Behind the static she heard a faint trickle of music. She cocked her head and strained to listen.

Paul Anka's "Having My Baby." She sat up, reached over and fiddled with the dial. The reception improved.

Kay's heart clutched at the sound of that voice she knew so well.

"I'll be standing in for Liam for the next couple of nights since Liam Junior got here. Hope you folks will bear with me. Since I'm at the controls and there's one hell of an aurora tonight, I'm going to be talking to a friend of mine, hoping she can hear me. Kay, baby, if you're out there, if you're listening, these next two are for you."

He played "New York, New York" and followed that with "Unforgettable."

She promptly burst into tears.

What on earth was she so scared of in Alaska? If she could live in Manhattan with the muggers and the pollution, why couldn't she make it in Alaska with a little darkness, a little cold weather, a few wild animals?

She missed that beautiful land. She missed Bear Creek. She missed the kind and welcoming townspeople.

And most of all, she missed Quinn.

What the hell was she doing in New York when everything she cared about was in Alaska?

THREE DAYS LATER Kay waited in line to board a plane bound for Anchorage. She was ready to begin her new life. She'd not only gone out on a limb, but sawn off the branch behind her. She'd sold off most of her belongings. And she'd quit her job at the magazine. Hal had been appalled at losing his best writer, but Judy had given her a thumbs-up and a ride out to JFK.

"Go get him, honey. He's a keeper," Judy had whispered in her ear as she gave her one last hug in the terminal before Kay passed through security.

The scary thing was, she hadn't spoken to Quinn. She was taking a huge chance, and she knew it. But if she'd learned anything from her first visit to Alaska, it was how to take a risk.

Thanks to Quinn.

Showing up unannounced had seemed like a terribly free-spirited, romantic, un-Kay-like thing to do. But now that everything was in motion, she started to panic.

Shifting the shoulder strap of her carry-on bag, she shuffled forward as the line moved. To distract herself from her anxiety, she studied the jetway neighboring her gate. A plane from Anchorage had just arrived and a gate agent moved to open the door. A steady stream of people began to disembark. From her peripheral vision, she caught sight of a tall, broad-shouldered man.

And did a double take.

Her heart thundered like a calving glacier.

Could it be him?

Nah.

Her line moved forward as her plane began to board. The big man in flannel and jeans was almost rounding the ticket counter. *Was* it him?

"Quinn!" she shouted, not caring that people stared. "Quinn!"

The man turned his head.

Gray eyes met hers. Recognition dawned. Then he stared in stunned disbelief.

"Kay?" A huge grin split his face.

He dropped his bag. She dropped hers.

She ducked under the roped-off area separating the departing passengers from their visitors.

He dodged a mother pushing a stroller.

In four, long-legged strides, he had her, catching her under the arms and swinging her high in the air as if she weighed no more than a toddler. Strong emotions surged through her—joy, excitement, wonderment.

And something else.

Love.

Quinn held her tightly to his chest. She could hear his heart pounding as heavily as her own.

Then he captured her mouth and kissed her.

Ah, the taste of him. How she'd missed his flavor!

"Isn't that sweet," someone in the crowd murmured.

"Makes me remember our courting days, Melinda," said someone else.

But it was all background noise to Kay, who only had eyes and ears for Quinn.

She kissed him hard and long. Kissed him in the airport terminal in front of dozens of openmouthed onlookers. She didn't care what anyone thought. She didn't care who she shocked or outraged. There was nothing wrong with expressing your love. And she refused to be ashamed of her physical urges any longer. He kissed her back until they were both gasping for air, and then he pulled away ever so slightly.

"What are you doing here?" she asked, at the same moment he said, "Where are you going?"

"I'm moving to Manhattan," he answered at the same moment she announced, "I'm moving to Bear Creek."

"What?" they cried in unison.

"Last boarding call for flight 1121 to Anchorage," intoned a voice over the loudspeaker.

Kay looked over her shoulder at the gate.

"You're not going now!" he exclaimed.

"No." She shook her head ruefully. "But everything I own is on its way to Alaska."

"And Meggie's staying in my cabin. Jesse's left her for an eighteen-year-old, and she's devastated. She's taken a leave of absence from her job, and she needed a place of her own to think things through."

"Oh," Kay said, genuinely sorry to hear about Meggie's trouble. "I feel so bad for her." As soon as she could, she'd give Meggie a call.

"It's been a long time coming." Quinn shook his head. "Jesse and Meggie were always too much alike to make a good couple."

"That's such a shame. Hadn't they been married a long time?"

''Six years. But let's not talk about Meggie's problems right now.'' He put his hand to Kay's back and ushered her toward a row of chairs. ''What happened to make you decide to move to Alaska?''

They sat down. His hand curled over hers. He couldn't seem to let go of her. It was as if he feared that without his hands on her body, she'd disappear.

She told him then about everything that had happened. Her realization that her family were snobs and would never change. How she'd confronted them about their attitudes and behaviors toward those less fortunate. How her parents had withdrawn from her after she'd expressed herself. She told him about being offered the head-writer position and not wanting it. About getting mugged. About reading Cammie Jo Lockhart's winning contest entry. And about hearing him dedicate those songs to her on the radio.

''I got the distinct impression the universe was trying to tell me something.''

''Sweetheart.'' He kissed her forehead.

''It was the mugging that made the biggest impression. I kept thinking that if something like that happened to me in Bear Creek—and what are the chances of that? A million to one?—the whole town would come to my rescue. Meggie would doctor my scrapes. You and Jake and Mack and Caleb would track him down. Even cantankerous old Gus would be there to lecture the guy when you captured him.''

''You're right about that.''

''I gave up my apartment. I quit my job. I wanted to go to Alaska. To come home. Quinn, Alaska has been in my blood and in my brain every since I left.

I couldn't stop thinking about Bear Creek, and I couldn't stop thinking about you.''

''Are you sure, Kay? You'd be giving up a lot. Success, social position, access to world-class shopping and cultural events. I can't offer you the kind of things your father can. But I can offer you respect and a sense of community, and most of all my love.''

''Oh, Quinn.'' She looked into his eyes. ''Yes, I'll be giving up a lot of *things.* But they're only things, after all. I'll be gaining my freedom and friendship, and most of all your love.''

''You really feel that way?''

Tears glistening in her eyes, she nodded. ''Can't you tell? But what about you? Look at the sacrifices you were willing to make for me. I can't believe you're moving to Manhattan. How were you planning to make a living?''

''Testing sporting equipment for Adventure Gear. I've already got a job.''

''What about your mountain-guide business?''

''I hired someone to manage it for me.''

''You'd be miserable in New York. This place would suffocate a wilderness man.''

He cupped her chin in his hand. ''No, it wouldn't. Not as long as I had you, sweetheart. It doesn't matter where we are as long as we're together. I decided I wasn't going to let my stubbornness get the best of me anymore. I have a problem with compromise. It's what came between me and my best friend Kyle. It's what came between me and Heather. After a lot of soul-searching, I realized I wasn't willing to give you up. This time I wasn't going to let pride and stubbornness keep me from the woman I love.''

"You want to tell me more about that?"

"I gave you a hard time about not expressing your feelings, but when push came to shove, I couldn't tell you what was in my heart. I was worried I wasn't good enough for a classy lady like you and too damned proud to admit it. Then I remember that because of my stubborn pride, I lost my friendship with Kyle."

"Oh?"

"I got angry with Kyle when he let Lisa wrap him around her little finger. It hurt when he chose her over me and Bear Creek. Lisa was the best thing that ever happened to Kyle, and he was smart enough to see it. I called Kyle recently and we talked for a long time. He made me see that I was throwing away a lifetime of happiness with you by being too set in my ways to change. I love Bear Creek, Kay, but I love you even more."

"You mean it?" Emotion clogged her throat. She laced her fingers through his.

"I love the soft, little snoring sound you make when you sleep. I love that scar below your ear. I love the way your brain works, the way you figure through problems intelligently and methodically. I love that you understand my need for independence. I love the way your body feels curled against mine. I love the way you look at me. As if I'm something."

"You are something." She was trembling. Trembling with a deep yearning for this man. "I want you so badly I ache, but I'm still scared."

"Fair enough," he murmured, and pulled her onto his lap. "You know the drill by now. Talk to me, babe. Tell me what's on your mind and in your heart. Don't hide your feelings from me. Lay them on the table."

"I'm afraid of bears," she whispered.

He threw back his head and laughed. "Whew! You had me going. I thought you were afraid of loving me."

"No! Not that. Loving you is the best thing that's ever happened to me."

"Well, don't you worry about those bears. We'll bear-proof our garbage cans, and I'll stock the house with bear repellent. You can wear bear bells wherever you go. I promise, honey, you're far more likely to get mugged in New York City than mauled in Bear Creek. Besides, you've got me to protect you."

It felt good to know that was true. She didn't need him for protection, but she wanted him. She was brave enough to make it on her own, but why should she have to when she had a man like Quinn?

"I'm so hot for you I can taste it," she whispered, running a finger along his lips. "Now let's find a hotel. When you made love to me, big man, you started something big."

TWENTY MINUTES LATER they were ensconced in a hotel room near the airport. Quinn tipped the bellboy, closed the door and turned to Kay with his best George-Clooney-on-the-make imitation.

"Come here, you." He crooked a finger at her.

Kay ran to him.

He whisked off her clothes, and to his utter delight discovered she was wearing a garter belt and those black seamed stockings underneath her blue jeans.

"You kill me, woman, you honestly do," he said, pinning her to the bed.

‘‘How so?’’

He raked his gaze over her body. ‘‘Those stockings,’’ he croaked. ‘‘Have you no idea the effect they have on a man?’’

Kay could feel his body heat radiating through her bare skin. Teasingly she turned her head and nipped at his wrist.

‘‘So take your clothes off,’’ she said, ‘‘and let’s make up for lost time.’’

‘‘Hang on. There’s something I’ve got to do first.’’

‘‘What?’’ She sighed, too hungry for him to wait any longer.

He rolled off her and perched on the edge of the bed. Kay sat up and tucked her legs beneath her. He reached into the pocket of his mackinaw and withdrew a small, black, velvet box.

‘‘Oh, my God!’’ Kay put her trembling hand to her mouth as Quinn cracked open the box with his thumb. A beautiful heart-shaped diamond ring in a platinum setting winked up at her.

‘‘I’d intended on waiting. After I got to New York. Found a place. Romanced you some more. But I can’t wait anymore. I put out an ad for a wild woman to become my wilderness wife. And from the moment I met you, even though I tried to deny it, I knew you were the one for me. Kay, you’re beyond my wildest dreams. I never believed I was good enough for you, but you’ve never made me feel that way. You’ve made me feel like twice the man I was before.’’

‘‘Oh, my God,’’ she repeated, staring into the depths of his eyes.

‘‘Will you marry me, Kay?’’

‘‘I can’t...I mean, I will...’’ Her hand was shaking

so badly she couldn't hold it still. Her stomach fluttered as if someone had let a million mad butterflies loose in it. "Oh, just let me show you."

She wrapped her arms around his neck and kissed him with all the passion she'd stored for just the right man to shower it upon. By taking a chance, by opening up and sharing her feelings, she found that intimacy she'd craved for so long.

"Is that a yes?" Quinn gasped a few minutes later.

"Yes."

He had to capture her hand at the wrist to hold it steady while he slipped the ring onto her finger. "Marry me in New York. Marry me today. Marry me now."

She shook her head. "No. Not today. I want to get married in Bear Creek. With all your family and friends. I'll marry you when we get home."

Home.

The band of emotion that had been getting tighter and tighter the closer he got to New York and Kay loosened, and his eyes stung with tears of hope and happiness.

"I love you, Kay, I always will. Now and forever. Here or in Bear Creek."

"And I love you." She touched his heart. "I can't wait to start steaming up those northern nights with you."

"I'm not waiting until we get back to Bear Creek for that."

In a flash Quinn shucked his clothes, lay down on the bed and pulled Kay on top of him.

"You know," she said as he planted kisses over her bare belly, "there are going to be a lot of disappointed women when they show up in Bear Creek and find there're only three eligible bachelors instead of four.''

''But think of the article possibilities,'' he said, and made a frame with his hands. ''I can see your title now—One Down, Three to Go. How I Landed the Wilderness Guide.''

''Well, it definitely needs some tweaking, but you just might have something there, big guy.''

''I'll show you what needs tweaking,'' he murmured, his tongue heading for a very sensitive place.

And the next thing Kay knew she was shooting into space with Quinn piloting the rocket, proving once and for all that she was indeed a very wild woman.

* * * * *

Does Cammie Jo Lockhart
have what it takes
to be a Wilderness Wife?

Be sure to watch for Cammie Jo
and Mack McCaulley's romance,
coming only to Duets in July 2002.

And now for a sneak preview,
please turn the page.

1

"FIRST TIME IN ALASKA," Mack McCaulley asked, to make conversation.

His passenger had yet to utter a single word. Even though it was summer, an overabundance of clothing almost swallowed her up.

In the ensuing minutes since takeoff, she had been staring at the floor, her hands clenched in white-knuckled terror.

"Uh-huh." She spoke so quietly Mack had to tilt his head and lean in her direction to hear. She had taken so long to respond he'd almost forgotten the question.

Thank heavens not all women who'd shown up in Bear Creek following their advertisement in *Metropolitan* magazine were this uncommunicative. Mack smiled at the thought of his last fare. A foxy redhead with a killer figure who'd pressed her cell-phone number into his hands and whispered, "Call me."

Now, *she* had seemed very adventuresome.

"But my mother was born in Alaska," Miss Marshmallow whispered after another silence so long he jumped when she spoke. "She was a bush pilot like you."

He almost didn't catch the last part. "For real."

The woman bobbed her head.

"Where's your mother from?"

"Fairbanks."

Well, that explained her overdressing. Fairbanks, nearer to the arctic circle, was much colder than the southern coastal region.

"So you're an Alaskan by proxy." He smiled.

"I guess so."

"Names Mack, by the way." He stuck out a hand. "Mack McCaulley."

"I know who you are. I recognized your picture from *Metropolitan* magazine. Page 110. The four of you guys are sitting around without shirts on."

"Ah, the infamous ad."

She stared at his chest then, as if recalling how bare he looked in that confounded advertisement, and her cheeks turned bright crimson.

Being here with Mack was too cool and too cruel, Cammie Jo thought. Of all the bush pilots in Alaska, how had she ended up with the object of her affections?

Of course, she hadn't the faintest notion of competing with other women to become this man's wife. Because of her shyness, she feared she would never find her true love the way her mother and father had found each other.

How she wished she was gutsy enough to flirt with him.

Ha! That'd be the day.

She knew Mack wasn't impressed with her. Men never were. He'd barely even glanced at her when she'd sidled up to where he stood in the airport, holding a placard with her last name written in a bold, masculine hand. Mack's gaze on her now was disconcerting. Frankly everything about him was disconcerting.

His outdoorsy, masculine scent. His husky, masculine voice. His stubble-darkened jawline.

And in his presence she was as nervous as a bunny rabbit at a hoot-owl jamboree.

I wish I was brave enough to have a real conversation with this man.

Nervously she stuffed her hand into her pocket, and her fingers glided over the treasured wish totem. It had belonged to her mother, and her aunts had given it to her before she'd left for Alaska. What if what they said was true and the necklace worked? She could wish for anything.

Bravery.

A husband.

True love.

How she wanted to believe in its mystical power. A power that would make her strong and brave. A power that would give her what it took to be a Wilderness Wife!